Kidnapping Casey

Zorn Warriors - Book Two

By Laurann Dohner

GW00676343

Kidnapping Casey
By Laurann Dohner

All Casey wants is to avoid being arrested on trumped-up charges from her persistent ex-boyfriend. Running through the woods to escape two deputies sounds like a great plan…until they catch her. Thinking it's all over, waiting to hear the snap of the handcuffs, she instead hears a roar.

A huge, tall, muscular man comes to her rescue. She's being saved by Bigfoot—and he's the sexiest thing she's ever seen. The attraction between them is instant, and after spending a little time with him, Casey wants to take him home and keep him.

There are a few problems with that plan. He's not the legendary creature, but he definitely isn't human. Argernon is a warrior from Zorn. They do have one thing in common—he wants to take her home and keep her. He's kidnapping Casey.

Zorn Warrior Series

Ral's Woman

Kidnapping Casey

Tempting Rever

Berrr's Vow

Coto's Captive

Kidnapping Casey

Copyright © June 2016

Editor: Kelli Collins

Cover Art: Dar Albert

ISBN: 978-1-944526-21-4

Chapter One

"No way in hell." Casey glared at the two deputies standing behind her car. "Don can drop dead."

Ben Harst sighed. "You know the drill after last week, Casey. Don't put up a fight. Don just wants to talk to you, so there's no reason to get all upset. We don't want to have to take you into town in handcuffs again." The man inched away from his patrol car, parked behind her vehicle in her driveway, staring up at Casey on her porch. "Just come along peacefully."

Greg Borrow nodded solemnly. "Don won't hurt you. He broke up with Donna and he just wants to talk. That's all."

Fear inched up Casey's spine. Donald Bass was the town sheriff—whom she'd broken up with six months ago when he'd cheated on her.

Just last week, he'd had his deputies arrest her in town. Don had almost raped her when she wouldn't take him back. If she hadn't screamed for help, she had no doubt that he wouldn't have stopped.

Don wasn't going to get his hands on her again. The guy was crazy.

"Leave me alone. You know he attacked me. Hell, Ben!" Her gaze flew to him. "*You* ran into his office when I screamed. He had me pinned down on his desk with my hands cuffed behind my back, taking my jeans down. I don't *want* him. I'd never take him back. He needs a damn shrink."

"He said you guys were role playing. I really don't want the details on your kinky sex life."

"Kinky sex life?" She gaped at Ben. "He tried to *rape me*. He had you arrest me. He wasn't taking no for an answer. Maybe you missed learning the actual law when you became a deputy, but it's illegal to force someone to have sex. You can't take me back to him."

"Sorry." Greg sighed. "We're under orders to arrest you."

"On what charge?" She backed up a few feet more. "You can't arrest me without charging me for a crime."

Greg and Ben glanced at each other. Ben turned his attention back to her. "You kicked him last week and he wants you arrested for assault."

Shock tore through her. "I was trying to make him stop pulling my pants down!"

"Well," Greg explained, "those are the charges. Now come here, Casey. We'll read you your rights and handcuff you real gentle. You know he'll drop the charges if you just hear him out."

"No."

Both men walked toward her porch.

Surprise hit Casey. They were actually going to arrest her again. After last week, she knew what Don was capable of. This time, she bet he'd send his deputies on some errand, so no one would be there to save her.

She fled into her house and slid the deadbolt into place. Casey wondered if they would really break into the house to come after her. She hoped not.

7

One of the deputies tested the knob, realizing it was locked when it wouldn't turn in his hand. Ben spoke. "Open the door, Casey, or we'll kick it in. Your car isn't going anywhere. You have nowhere to run. You know you'll take him back."

"No. I won't!" she yelled out and backed up more. "I know he's a sick jerk now. He can go to hell!"

Alarm tore through her when one of them kicked the door hard. She heard the wood crack but it held.

She ran through her living room and as she reached the kitchen, the front door crashed open, hitting the wall.

Hatred for Don poured through her. Casey was so over his ass, it wasn't funny.

What she'd ever seen in the handsome son of a bitch...

Yeah, she thought, *there was that.* He was eye candy who could charm a nun out of her underwear, but any good aspects of him died when he'd cheated.

She flew down the back porch steps. She'd lived in the woods all of her life, and ran for them now at full speed. If she could just get down by the river, she knew they wouldn't be able to find her. Dozens of hiding places there flashed through her mind.

Boots pounded behind her. Being five feet five wasn't to her advantage in a race when everyone was taller and had longer legs. Sprinting wasn't her strong suit, she decided, as she dodged trees to avoid slamming into them.

Ben cursed as he ran with Greg, both breathing heavily as they pursued her.

One of them grabbed her long, dark brown hair like a tether. Casey screamed out in pain as she was yanked abruptly to a halt.

She felt a heavier body hit her from behind when Ben was unable to stop in time, and the three of them crashed facedown to the ground in a heap.

Ben wasn't exactly a fit deputy; he was more the donut-loving variety, so his body crushed her hard enough to knock the air from her lungs when he landed on her. Pain sliced through her body as the man shifted his frame on her smaller one. Someone gripped her wrist, yanking it painfully behind her back.

"Damn," Ben panted, "I can't believe you made us chase you."

Dragging air into her lungs, Casey screamed. She managed to yank her hand out of Ben's hold as she fought. The deputy cursed when she swung an elbow back and nailed him. Another scream tore free as both men grabbed her, pinning her to the ground on her belly.

"Stop fighting, damn it! Don't make us hurt you," Greg yelled as he grabbed her flailing wrist, using his knee to push her hip against the ground.

Pain made her scream again. The knee painfully dug into her as he put weight on her ass. She saw him reach for his handcuffs.

Movement from behind Greg made her gaze fly in that direction—

And astonishment made her stop struggling altogether when a huge man ran out of the trees.

No way.

He moved fast but she couldn't miss that body—and her mind struggled to process the sight before her. Long black hair flowed in disarray down to his waist. He looked *huge*. Black leather encased most of his deeply tanned body. The long hair whipped around his face, covering most of his features. With his head lowered as well, Casey couldn't see him clearly.

The form-fitting material covering the stranger embraced wide shoulders and really muscular arms, the outfit showing off his massive chest and trim waist to perfection. Thick, muscular thighs were showcased in pants that tapered down strong calves to some kick-ass heavy black boots that looked made to do serious damage.

The two deputies still hadn't looked behind them, so Casey was the only one who saw that massive man coming. He was almost on top of them before a roar tore through the woods, making Ben, Greg and Casey jump.

The deputies spun, staring up at their worst nightmare, right before the man grabbed both of them with his huge hands.

Ben's body was thrown at a tree—literally. The large stranger sent the overweight deputy flying a good ten feet as if he were a toy. Ben hit the tree with a crunch and a loud groan that made Casey cringe as he slumped to the ground. His leg moved weakly but he didn't get up.

The stranger then lifted Greg by the front of his shirt. Casey had rolled over to see the deputy dangling in the stranger's grasp. The long-haired man snarled deeply, revealing sharp teeth when his full lips parted.

A high-pitched scream came from Greg, making him sound like a terrified little girl.

A stunned Casey could only watch as the scene played out before her. Greg was a good six feet tall, yet the stranger held him almost half a foot off the ground—putting them nose to nose. The man viciously snarled at Greg again before tossing him away, sending him to the ground with a grunt.

Casey didn't turn her head to see how Greg fared, terror kept her staring up at the huge man standing over her.

She got a much better look at the man's face when he gazed at her.

And he *was* male, she knew that instantly, but what hit her the hardest was the clear fact he wasn't fully human. This man had a wider, flatter nose than anyone she'd ever seen before. The scary teeth peeking out of his full lips reminded her of a dog's long canines. He looked like a vampire, with those sharp fangs indenting his lower lip, except is was broad daylight so she doubted that theory.

His eyes were startling. Once her gaze met his, she couldn't look away. If she had any doubts he wasn't human, they were gone now.

His eyes were an unnaturally bright electric-blue that almost glowed. Long, thick black eyelashes framed them, making the blue stand out even more. They were absolutely the most spellbinding things she'd ever seen.

11

He took a deep breath before his lips slammed shut. The action drew Casey's gaze back to his mouth. A set of masculine lips tightened into a firm line before he bent over and reached for her.

Casey wanted to scream. She wanted to roll away, but she just couldn't move. Disbelief had her frozen.

His tan fingers were hot as they wrapped around her, arms just under her shoulders. His touch was firm but undeniably gentle as he pulled her off the ground slowly. There was no doubt that he was strong, since she didn't help him lift her at all. She was too bewildered to get her body to work.

Her legs barely held her weight when he stood her on her feet, making her realize that the top of her head didn't even reach his wide shoulders, a good foot in height separated them. His firm hands held her while she stared in wonder at those amazing eyes that hypnotized her with their exotic beauty.

Their gazes remained locked until he finally looked away, but Casey's attention stayed on him as he studied the two downed men. Their gazes met again when he swung his head back to her. Thick masculine lips parted slightly and he growled at her.

"Oh God," she breathed. "What are you?"

A softer, nonthreatening growl came from him. She would have screamed if his tone was vicious, but she got the distinct sense he was trying to communicate with her.

The truth sunk in slowly.

"You can't speak, can you?" She cleared her throat when it threatened to close up on her from the lump that formed.

Frustration was clear on his rugged face. He had a strong jawline, pronounced cheekbones and his wide, flat nose twitched. Those incredible eyes narrowed in irritation. With the shake of his head, she had her answer.

"You know English? Do you know what I'm saying?"

He nodded.

"Are you a girl?"

A growl tore from his throat in instant protest. Anger sparked in his glowing stare as he shook his head. His fingers tightened for an instant before loosening again on her skin.

"I was just checking to see if you can really understand me. I know you're a boy." She had to swallow again. Her throat was dry, her heart pounding. "What are you?"

He looked at her for what seemed like forever.

Then suddenly the man's intensely strange but gorgeous gaze tore from hers to could look over her head. His mouth opened as a low growl came from his throat. It was a scary, vicious sound. Rage filled his expression in a heartbeat. His flat nose wrinkled and sharp teeth showed as his lips parted wider. His hold on Casey tightened almost painfully when his fingers tensed.

Greg cursed from behind her.

Casey swung her head around. Sitting up, Greg looked terrified while gawking at the large male who held her. His shaking hands went for his sidearm.

"No!" Casey yelled. "Don't shoot him!"

Greg ignored her, yanking at the gun in his holster. It took him a few tugs to clear it and then he was wildly waving the weapon in their direction, his hands shaking.

Casey was horrified at what was happening but felt helpless to stop it.

Hands slowly released Casey's arms, moving lower to her hips.

Then she was jerked off her feet and the world went upside down in less than a heartbeat, the fast movement making her dizzy.

A gunshot exploded with a deafening crack.

But by that time, the man gripping Casey was already running, his arm locked behind her knees, holding her tightly.

He moved *really* fast.

Casey was folded over his body, her hips nestled tightly against the man's shoulder. It didn't hurt, but the position jarred the breath from her lungs as she bounced against him. The ground passed beneath her at an alarming rate but she couldn't even scream.

Another gunshot exploded in the woods but the boom wasn't even close.

They were weaving through the trees, toward the river, the man leaving no tracks to follow, despite his boots. Greg shouted in the distance but they were already too far away for Casey to hear what he was saying. She guessed he was calling for backup.

Was Ben dead? She'd heard something crack when Ben had hit the tree. Was it his body or the tree that had made that sickening noise?

Casey pushed the thought away. She needed to worry about her own ass.

The large male creature continued to put distance between them and the two men they'd left behind. The men who'd tried to cuff and arrest her…

Now, Casey was being kidnapped.

She was afraid of the stranger dropping her when he eventually exhausted himself by hauling her extra weight, but he didn't slow down at all. Whatever he was, he was damn strong, since he seemed to be able to run for miles. Harsh breathing was the only indication that carrying her was any sort of strain.

They finally slowed to a walk as the sound of water reached her ears. She lifted her head, shoving at her hair to get it out of her face. She looked around and instantly recognized the large rock formation to her left. She could also hear the river just behind her, and Casey knew exactly where they were on her property; almost on the border of one of her neighbors'. A forty-foot waterfall pounded into the river just ahead. She knew the place well. It was one of her favorite places to swim.

The man stopped to sniff the air as he studied the area. Slowly bending, he loosened his hold around her legs and his other hand braced her back as he put her down. He released her but didn't step away.

Casey could only stare up at the man, still speechless.

His hand gently grabbed her wrist and his head jerked toward the water.

She turned to glance at the water cascading down into the narrower river near where they stood. He squeezed her hand gently to draw her attention to him.

"You want me to go into the water?"

He nodded.

"You really can't talk?"

He shook his head.

Her heart pounded in her chest. "Shit."

He motioned his head in the direction of the water again.

Casey took a deep breath before walking toward the river. The male kept hold of her wrist, moving with her to the water's edge. She stopped to look up at him and noticed again that he was a huge son of a bitch. He had to be six feet five or six at least.

"I could use a drink." She tugged on her wrist.

He frowned, shaking his head, pointing to the waterfall. Frowning back, she met his exceptional eyes. She wasn't sure what he wanted her to do, why he wanted her to go into the river.

Irritation crossed his features. With a swift jerk, her body abruptly collided with his much larger one. Before she could protest, she'd ended up back in his arms. He lifted her against his chest, cradled in his arms, and then he walked into the water, heading toward the waterfall.

Apprehension filled Casey. Was he going to drown her? She wrapped her arms tightly around his neck as the water got really deep. He continued forward until the water touched her chin, and then stopped. Their gazes locked as he released her legs.

She felt the pull of the current, and would have floated away if he wasn't holding her against his chest. She eased her arms from his neck to grip his shoulders. They were face-to-face, with only inches separating their noses.

Casey studied his features curious but still cautious. He was handsome, she realized. Tan skin covered his strong, masculine features. His lips looked a little pouty, making them appear sexy. The shape of his nose was strange but somehow it looked good on him, and she had the strange urge to run her fingers over it. With the tiny lines by his eyes, he had the appearance of someone in his mid-thirties, just a few years older than her.

Her stare met his again. He studied her with curiosity too. She saw it sparkling in his extraordinary eyes.

He pointed to the waterfall. Her gaze followed his finger before she looked back at him. He growled at her in that soft tone she was starting to think was just a little sexy.

"You want me to swim for the waterfall?"

He nodded.

"Why?"

Irritation flashed again on his face. He brought a hand up to make a rounded claw with it, motioning. He pointed to the waterfall again, and sudden realization dawned on her.

"You know about the cave behind it, don't you? Do you want us swim there to climb into the cave?"

He nodded. The frustration faded from his features and his arm around her back loosened. He jerked his head toward the waterfall once more before looking back at the embankment. He growled, seemingly trying to communicate something to her, and she glanced at the woods.

He must be worried about the deputies following them. No one knew about the cave, however—and Casey wondered how *this* guy had discovered it.

He released her totally so she could make her way to where he wanted her to go.

Casey didn't want to be found either. Getting arrested wasn't on her list of things she ever wanted to do again, not to mention being alone with Don.

She paddled against the current, heading for the waterfall, her clothes heavy as she swam. The river got deep enough that the bottom was untouchable even for the stranger, so he swam close behind her.

The worst part about going to the cave was swimming under the pounding waterfall, which tore at her clothing and tried to push her deep under the surface. Casey was relieved when she cleared the heavy curtain of water to reach the other side.

It was dim behind the screen of water but she could see well enough to make out the area. Clawing at the rocks, she climbed out of the water toward the mouth of the cave, which sat about four feet over her head. The stranger surfaced from under the waterfall just as she'd crawled into the rocky cave. It wasn't very big, but was at last dry about five feet or so inside the entrance. She scrambled away from the wet ledge, deeper into the cave, and then sat on her ass to watch as the guy followed.

His attention was focused on Casey.

With his wet hair plastered back, she got another good look at his face. Yes, his features were definitely human-like, though his nose was definitely wrong, and the thick-lipped mouth and those fangs were inhuman as well. In the darkened cave, his eyes looked eerie as they seemed to glow in the dim light.

He pointed behind her, so she turned, taking a good look at the interior of the cave as her eyes adjusted further. Surprise struck her, seeing what she'd previously missed.

She hadn't been in the cave in a while. Now, several more feet back, there was a sleeping bag spread out along the back wall, with a backpack of sorts next to it. Casey returned her attention to the man.

"Are you living here?"

A nod confirmed her suspicion.

He reached for the front of his shirt, spreading the material open, revealing substantial muscles covered by more tanned skin. She was too taken aback to do anything but watch as the man removed his shirt completely. Casey stared at his chest, noting that he was a little hairy

19

there, but it wasn't excessive. A thin line of it ran below his belly button to disappear into those form-fitting pants...

His big hands reached for the waist of while he toed off his boots.

Silently, he observed Casey as she observed him right back. There was no question, she decided, that he had the best damn body she'd ever seen. He looked one hundred percent powerfully built human from the neck down. She'd never seen a better-defined body. Each muscle was ripped. The front of his pants was now open, hinting at more golden-brown skin there. That thin black trail of hair continued down his lower belly.

Casey couldn't tear her eyes away from the sight of him slowly lowering the leather material that clung to his skin. The pants inched down as he wiggled his hips. A gasp escaped her when his penis sprang free.

He was aroused.

Casey's mouth fell open. He was thick, most definitely hard, and his cock was shaped slightly different from a human's. The skin of his shaft was a reddish hue, which was human enough, as far as aroused males went. But the head was thick, more of a distinct, exaggerated mushroom shape than the smooth transition from head to shaft most guys had.

And he was proportioned to his big body.

In fact, she'd never seen a guy that big. Not that she had much to compare him to. Her few ex-boyfriends had been pricks in every sense of the word.

Her body responded instantly as she continued to stare at his anatomy. Uncharacteristically, she wondered how it would feel as he slowly worked that thick, blunt tip inside her.

Her pussy clenched in response to the image that flashed in her mind. Moisture flowed between her thighs. She slammed her mouth shut and jerked her gaze upward to his face.

A twinkle of amusement sparked in his sexy eyes and his lips curved upward into a knowing grin. She flushed a little, heat flaming her face as she prayed he couldn't read what she'd been thinking.

When his pants were completely off, his hand rose, one finger extended to point at her. She blinked a few times, forcing air into her lungs, as it sank in what he must want her to do.

"Oh hell. I'm not getting naked too."

He softly growled at her and his grin died. Glowing blue eyes narrowed before he stalked closer. His body was graceful, powerful, and his muscles moved with lithe beauty. She was fascinated by every damn inch of his skin.

He moved so close that her eyes flew down to his cock again. A thick vein ran from the base of his shaft to just under the mushroomed head. She was close enough to touch the swollen flesh that pointed straight at her.

He slowly crouched, his face getting closer. Her breath froze in her lungs, her heart pounded as desire shot through her. Would he want to fuck her?

His erection certainly indicated he did, if he was anything like normal men.

Large hands reached for her, encircling her arms above her elbows. He pulled her to her feet in a heartbeat, rising with her. Her knees almost collapsed when he forced her to stand. His intense gaze glided down her body, seeming to take in every inch, and a sexy, soft noise came from his parted lips before his hands released her.

She took a deep breath—until those hands went for the waist of her T-shirt.

The wet material was swiftly ripped up her body.

Casey tried to turn away but he was faster. One arm wrapped around her waist to pull her tightly against him. She was chilled from being in the cold river, but his body was hot to the touch. His hard erection pressed into her bared stomach as the shirt went sailing to the cave floor. Her bra-covered breasts were smashed against his muscular chest.

He breathed her in, another sexy growl tearing from his parted lips, and his cock jerked against her belly. He was so incredibly hard.

"Please don't hurt me."

He frowned, shaking his head, a frustrated look crossing his features. His chest rose as he took a deep breath, their bodies pressing even more tightly together. Long seconds ticked by while Casey's heart beat erratically in her chest. His hold eased until a foot of space opened between them. His cock wasn't touching her now but he didn't let her arm go.

His gaze lowered between them to his protruding member.

Casey's eyes followed. This up close and personal, she realized just how thick his cock was. Her previous interest at the thought of him working that inside her was now tinged with a little fear.

He shook his head at her when she jerked her attention back to his eyes. His hand slowly released her to point at the bedding.

"What in the hell are you trying to tell me?"

He backed up farther, pointed to her remaining clothing. That long digit went to his bedding next as he mimicked covering up. Slowly he turned around to present his wide back to her.

The man moved away, closer to the mouth of the cave, still facing the falling water and keeping his back to Casey.

She stood there shivering. Some of her fear eased when she realized he was giving her privacy. Her gaze kept going to his body as she stripped out of the rest of her clothes. He had the nicest damn butt ever. Broad shoulders tapered down to his toned back and to that fantastic ass. She shook herself from thoughts of what it would feel like to rake her fingernails down the length of him.

Slowly turning to his sleeping bag, she climbed in it to cover up her freezing body. The bedding was thick and warm and Casey relaxed, quickly warming up enough to stop shivering. She eyed his wide back and great ass again. He really was perfect; she'd never seen a man in better shape than he was in.

A good three minutes passed before the man finally turned around. He walked over to their clothing on the floor, bending to retrieve them one piece at a time.

Casey silently watched him lay them out over rocks so they would dry. His hard-on had gone down. Even soft, the sensual flesh hanging between his thighs, the guy was impressive.

Finally he turned to face her.

She had to give him credit; he seemed totally at ease with his nakedness.

Her breath sped as he slowly inched closer. Crouching down next to the sleeping bag, he tilted his head slightly to study her, his beautiful eyes narrowed. He watched her face for a long minute as their gazes remained locked.

It came as a shock when the large man suddenly lunged.

Chapter Two

Fear hit the instant he touched her. He firmly pushed, hands on her shoulders, until Casey was forced flat onto her back. The bedding was torn from her fingers and jerked away from her body. He trapped her under him as his naked body came down on top of her smaller one. Large hands gripped her wrists to jerk them above her head; he forced his legs between her thighs to push them wide apart. She was spread-eagle under the man, pinned there firmly, with their noses almost touching.

He shut his eyes, sniffing at her for a few seconds before his face turned sideways, inching closer to her until his warm nose brushed her throat. A soft growl rumbled from deep in his chest. Against her inner thigh, she felt his cock harden again as blood flooded it. Smelling her was obviously turning him on.

"Please don't hurt me." Casey hated the frightened quiver in her voice.

His eyes glowed brighter, desire and something primal showing in them. He shook his head, frowning, watching Casey. It was obvious he wanted to say something to her but she couldn't understand. Another growl rumbled from his parted lips, his chest vibrating slightly where it pressed down on her bared breasts, making her more aware of her hardening nipples. Growls were obviously how he talked—and she didn't speak "growl." As frustration flashed on his face, Casey could relate.

Electric-blue eyes closed as he lowered again to her neck. His breath was hot against her skin, making Casey shiver a little at the sensation. He inhaled slowly and deeply, an erotic awareness going through her as his nose lightly caressed the line of her throat. He seemed to *really* like the way she smelled, judging by the major hard-on pressed against her. He wasn't hurting her though or forcing her to have sex with him—yet. Their gazes clashed when his head rose.

Releasing her wrists, he lifted his chest a little from her body, and she missed his warmth as he separated them from their stomachs up. His body temperature was hotter than a normal man's. A smile twisted his lips when his eyes lowered to her exposed breasts.

Casey wasn't sure what that smile meant, but she could guess. She tensed. The thought of fighting him crossed her mind, but she knew she'd never get someone his size off her. She felt tiny, caged there under his expansive chest and between the thickly muscled arms braced on both sides of her ribs.

She gasped when he dipped his head, sliding down so his hard cock moved away from her mound and inner thigh, and his hot mouth opened over her right nipple. His tongue slid out to touch her. The man licked the crest of her breast, softly growling at her again. He sucked the bud into his mouth.

A jolt shot through her body as his slightly raspy tongue teased around her hardening peak. He sucked on her breast, pulling more of her inside that hot mouth of his, his sharp teeth clamped down on her tender flesh. There was no pain but he had a good grip on her, between his teeth and the suction of his mouth.

Held immobile by the amazing sensation of what he was doing to her body, Casey's shock was replaced by awareness of her desire rising—and a keen sense of self-preservation. Gathering her scattered wits, she began frantically pushing at his chest with her hands. His tense muscles felt like steel as she pressed hard, trying to move him, but he wouldn't budge or release her breast. Instead, he doubled his efforts, suckling and biting, her struggles ceasing as hard tugs of his mouth on her nipple sent sparks throughout her body.

The sensation wasn't like anything she'd ever experienced before. She'd had a few lovers in her life—four, to be exact—but not one of them had sucked on her as roughly he was. His teeth scraped her nipple, causing her to squirm, that hot mouth making her ache between her thighs. It felt like as if her breast was connected directly to her pussy.

Her clit started to throb under the man's frontal assault. Her hands went from pushing at his chest to sliding up to his shoulders, where she clutched the curve of them. She felt her vaginal walls twitch, wetness flooding her, as the ache became a burning need. Her nails dug into his skin, a moan bursting from her lips, her hips arching unbidden into his stomach.

The man was relentless with that mouth. He finally released her hard peak with a soft sound before slowly moving to the neglected breast. Casey hated the way she lifted her back so her breast pushed against his mouth as he started suckling again, but her body had a will of its own.

He shifted his hips, sliding down her a little more, even as her fingernails clawed at him, trying to pull him back up. She was throbbing with a need that consumed her. The guy might look part animal, but he was bringing out the animal in *her* even more. She wanted him to work his cock inside her where she was soaked...where she ached to the point of pain.

She suddenly wished she knew his name. He obviously couldn't tell her, unless in some growling that she doubted she could mimic.

As he released her breast, cool air hit her wet nipple. She felt it pucker almost painfully in the chilly cave. Her gaze flew to his incredible glowing stare and she saw a look of intense, burning hunger in those eyes. Casey wondered if she looked as turned-on as he did.

He pushed up off her body, inhaling deeply as he slid farther down. She realized what he had in mind when his attention moved away from her brown eyes, past her belly and to her exposed sex.

She tried to shut her thighs but he was faster. He crouched between her legs, gripping them with both, the rough skin of his palms exhilarating as he coaxed her to open wider. He took one deep breath to inhale her scent.

A small cry escaped her as he buried his face between her legs.

She would have screamed louder from the instant surprise of a man's tongue diving into her sex, but the hot, thick tongue swiping through her pussy and breaching her entrance stole her breath. He pushed his tongue deep inside her, a snarl tearing from his throat. Normally that vicious sound would have terrified her, but he made it literally impossible to fear him at the moment.

She threw her head back, trying to squeeze her thighs together for an entirely different reason now, but his hands held her open. All she managed to do was push her pussy tighter against his face. He growled again, a new sensation that had her moaning as the sound vibrated against her.

Then he discovered her clit—and she froze completely, forgetting to even breathe, as his tongue teased it lightly.

"Oh God. Yes!"

Casey definitely didn't want him to stop now. She threw her arms above her head clawing at his bedding, her back arching off his sleeping bag. She felt pure rapture when he licked her clit, focusing on the oversensitive bud. She stopped trying to slam her thighs shut. She shamelessly spread them wider to give him easier access, her hips jerking slightly.

"Faster, please," she begged softly. "That feels so good."

He understood her. He increased the pace, getting a good hold and sucking on her clit with steady tugs as his lips sealed over the entire nub. She felt sharp teeth slightly gripping, but they didn't hurt her and he continued to rub his tongue rapidly against her clit.

Casey hadn't had sex in a long time. After six months of only touching herself, she was ready to explode. She didn't even try to hold back.

She came hard, crying out as she jerked against his relentless mouth. Her head thrashed from side to side as she kept coming while he

29

continued to play with her swollen nub. Her cries turned to a whimper when she became oversensitive.

He released her slowly. Casey felt like a marionette whose tight strings had been cut. She went limp on his bedding—until he drove his tongue inside her pussy without warning. She gasped as he wiggled that strong organ back and forth, pushing against her inner walls, sucking on her. She tried to slam her thighs around his head but his hands pushed them open again.

His tongue slid out of her slowly as he released small growls. Casey closed her eyes, spent, as he slid up her body, moving between her spread legs. His hot, muscled frame pinned her smaller one under his, but she knew he was being careful to not crush her with his heavier weight, since she could easily breathe. One of his hands gripped her calf, pushing it up so her heel was level with his hip.

When she finally looked at him, blue eyes seem to glow right into her soul.

The rounded tip of his cock pressed against her pussy—and then Casey moaned as she felt him pushing inside her body.

He was huge, and she knew the head of his shaft was thicker than anything she'd ever taken. There was resistance as her body tried to fit him. He was patient, sinking into her so, so slowly, burying himself deep until she felt stretched to the limit.

Their gazes met.

The man growled softly at her, the sound sexy when uttered during such profound intimacy. He started to move, withdrawing a few inches, only to push gently back into her. She experienced new, wonderful sensations as he filled her at a leisurely pace. Her muscles still quivered from her previous climax.

Without thought, she released his bedroll to wrap her arms around his neck.

Casey couldn't look away from him. He was almost beautiful with pleasure etched on his features, his mouth slightly parting as his passion-filled gaze fell to her lips. She knew he wanted to kiss her.

She leaned up to offer her mouth, hoping those sharp teeth of his wouldn't hurt. When their lips met, her eyes closed.

The kiss was *not* slow.

Almost savagely, he dominated her mouth. She met his kiss and matched his passion. He began to move faster inside her, with more force, the sensations making her moan into his mouth. She loved the way he took possession of her, his full lips locked over hers, his tongue imitating the motion of his cock.

It was sensory overload as he built speed until his cock pounded in and out of her in rhythm with his kiss.

She tore her mouth away from his as another climax hit her. Pleasure tore through her body, her fingernails digging into his back as her hips jerked violently under his.

Casey felt him tense, his body going rigid, before he drove deeper into her. His movements became frantic just before his cock throbbed against her vaginal walls and he came with a roar. She felt him pulsing, his semen spilling into her.

He buried his face in her neck as he growled softly, saying something she couldn't understand. They were both breathing hard and sweat trickled between their bodies. She felt his heart pounding against her breast. Casey remembered that her nails were digging into the flesh on his back, so she eased her grip.

The man on top of her finally lifted his head.

Long hair fell around them like a curtain, making the moment just that much more intimate. Their gazes met and Casey stared at him in wonder. She suddenly remembered a song about wanting to be fucked like an animal. She just *had* been—and it had been the best damn sex she'd ever had in her life.

"I wish I knew your name," was all she could think to say.

She almost had the urge to thank him. Her body felt more sated than it ever had. She felt zero urge to make him move off her. She just wanted to stay this way, with him pinning her under his hot body, with his cock still buried deep inside her. Having him on top of her felt right, like he belonged there, their bodies fitting together perfectly.

A small smile played at his lips. He winked at her. Pushing up off her chest, he braced his weight with one hand while he touched her breast with his other, cupping the entire globe in his large hand. His rough-textured palm slid over her tender skin, the sensation pleasant enough that she pressed against that hand, seeking more. He released her before gripping his chest over his heart. A soft, sexy growl rumbled from him. He cupped her breast again and then his chest.

She stared at him, wondering what he was trying to say.

"Breast to breast?"

Chuckling, he shook his head. Amusement lit his already bright eyes. He lowered his body back on top of Casey to pin her there firmly. They admired each other for a long time. His smile faded slowly as he lowered his head and his lips brushed hers softly. Casey shut her eyes to kiss him back.

This time they weren't two frantically turned-on people coming together. This kiss was tender and long. He was exploring her mouth, learning her, and to Casey, it felt even a little teasing, playful.

While he had possession of her lips, he started to move inside her again.

Astonishment hit Casey...but so did desire. His cock was still rock hard.

She knew he'd come, she'd felt him. He recovered way too fast to be human, just another reminder of how *not* normal he was. She didn't even want to think about the no-condom thing. Maybe he couldn't carry sexual diseases.

She wasn't worried about pregnancy, though. She'd worked for a veterinarian for two years before she'd started bartending school, and she knew different species couldn't breed. She was fully human and he was...something else entirely. They were cats and dogs, pretty much, no matter how similar. Or so she told herself. They might be sexually compatible but they sure couldn't make babies.

He broke away from her mouth. She missed his kiss instantly but she quickly got over it as he went for her neck and the top of her shoulder.

Sharp teeth raked her flesh. It was an erotic sensation that drew her desire to a higher level. He could hurt her with those teeth, but instead he was gently scraping along her skin. Gut instinct assured her she was safe with this man.

He moved languidly, driving her desire up again. She raked her fingernails along his back and shoulders where she could reach while she lifted her legs higher, wrapping them tightly around his waist. Her heels pressed into his firm ass. Strong muscles there worked, tightening as he slowly fucked her.

"Oh God," she moaned. "Faster, please. I like it fast."

He growled before he drove into her the way she wanted. Casey moaned, quaking under him. He was a powerhouse of sex. She pushed that thought away to just feel.

Sharp teeth nipped her shoulder hard enough to bring her a flash of pain. It shocked her but didn't really hurt. He hadn't pierced her skin. It *did* excite her body into a climax, pleasure thrummed through her as she cried out.

The large man groaned deeply next to her ear. She felt him throb, her muscles milking his cock as he emptied himself deep inside her again.

They both stilled except for their heavy breathing. Minutes passed before he slowly withdrew from her body.

Casey felt awed by her licentious responses to him. She opened her eyes...

Only to see regret shining in that strangely beautiful blue stare.

He pushed away from her upper body and Casey released his hips, unwinding her legs from around him. They shook from the workout she'd gotten. She fought sleep as he sat back on his heels between her thighs, taking her in.

She wondered why he looked so regretful. He couldn't be regretting the sex…could he? After all, they'd done it twice—and it had been amazing.

Touching his chest, he pointed to hers. His mouth curved upward. He had a sexy smile. Casey bit her lip as she eased up carefully, using her hands to brace her weight. She couldn't close her thighs with him sitting between them but she did move back a few inches so there was a little distance between his knees and her exposed pussy. She sat up straighter to stare at him on a more equal level.

"I wish I understood you." She touched her chest. "I'm Casey Santhrom. I live in a house close to here. I own this." She waved her hands at the cave. "I own the land." Her hands dropped as she studied him. He was watching her intently.

"You can understand me, right?"

He nodded slowly with a smile.

She smiled back. "You really can't say words?"

He shook his head. A soft growl came from his parted lips.

"Okay. Can you write to tell me your name?"

Amusement lit his eyes. His lips twitched. He shook his head.

Disappointment hit her. She was hoping maybe he could spell words to her in the loose dirt of the cave floor. At least that would have been some form of communication. Studying his features, taking in the human face with slight animal characteristics, a grim thought hit her.

"*Shit*. Some asshole doctor did this to you, didn't he? Is that what happened to make you so different? Was some geneticist experimenting on you? Did you escape some laboratory? God! That shit is illegal. We'll get you help." Her eyes flashed up and down his body. "We won't let them get away with this. Were they experimenting on you with some kind of animal DNA?"

The grin widened as he shook his head.

"No? I'm not right?" She racked her brain for a moment—then the blood drained from her face. Fear inched up her spine and her eyes ran over him again as a local legend she'd heard throughout childhood flooded back.

"Oh shit. I know what you are."

A black eyebrow arched. His eyes sparkled as he continued to grin, his amusement clear as he silently watched her.

She was glad he was amused. *She* wasn't.

"You're a Big Foot! I thought they were furry but...maybe not all of them? I mean, you have that crazy-long hair on your head, and some chest hair, but what else could you be? A few were supposedly spotted in this area back in the sixties and seventies. Obviously not you. You're too young. Maybe it was your parents. Oh! Or maybe your human mom or dad mated with one somehow? Are you a Big Foot?"

His body shifted so he sat down on his ass at the bottom of the bedding. He raised a bare foot for her inspection. He had really big ones. She swallowed.

"Big hands, big feet…" Her eyes darted to his spread thighs. He was still semi-erect. "Big…*everything*. Hot damn! You're a Big Foot! Wow, this is both cool and, um…slightly mortifying. Oh my God. You really *do* exist. And—"

He laughed cutting off her rant.

Casey smiled back, wondering how he'd learned to understand English, but she could guess. He'd obviously lived in the woods all of his life, and plenty of people were around. He must have watched and learned to understand them.

She studied him again. He looked like he was in his mid-thirties. He seemed smart; he had intelligent eyes. He probably stayed out of sight because the world would make his life a circus, between people wanting to gawk at him, the media wanting to exploit him…and doctors and scientists would probably die for a chance to study him literally to death.

"So are there any female Big Foot women nearby?"

He shook his head. The twinkle left his eyes. Casey mourned the loss almost immediately. The guy was cute as hell when he was amused. When not amused, he looked intimidating with his intense stare. She didn't really fear him, not after they'd shared sex. He'd saved her from Ben and Greg too. She sensed he was no danger to her.

He must have moved to the cave recently. He sure hadn't lived there last summer, the last time she'd been in it. Maybe he lived like a nomad, traveling around from one thickly wooded area to the next so he wasn't detected. She wondered if he'd even been in a house before. Did he know what a television was? Modern plumbing? Surprising sadness hit her. To live the way he did must be hard. She swallowed the lump in her throat.

"You can come home with me. I live in a remote area. I live alone. You'd be safe there. I work a lot and I don't have much time for friends anymore, so no one will bother us."

A soft growl rumbled from him. He pointed to the falling water.

Casey following his finger, nodding. She was pretty sure he wanted to know what had happened out there.

"I don't know if you'll understand all of this but I dated a guy. He slept with another woman six months ago. I caught him with his pants down—literally. I broke it off with him. Now the woman he cheated on me with just broke up with him, too, so he's trying to get me back. Last year he was elected sheriff…that basically means he's in charge of this area. He sent those two goons who work for him to my house to get me. He thinks he can force me to be with him, that I'll just take him back.

"But don't worry. I'll handle him somehow, and get him to leave me alone. Hopefully those men won't be back. You should come live with me. I have modern technology. I think you'd like television and hot showers. You won't have to hunt for your food anymore. I can just buy it at the grocery store. I'm a bartender, so I don't have a lot of money, but I make good tips and get by just fine. I can afford to feed you as long as you don't eat a ton of food." She smiled.

Laughing, he looked down his body then cocked a brow at her.

She raked her gaze over him, laughing as well. "Okay. You're big. We can supplement a little with some hunting. I own a lot of land. I can skin a rabbit and I make a great stew. It's also good on the grill. We have a river to fish from. But what I'm saying is, you don't have to live like this anymore. I can protect you and teach you how to read and write. That way you can talk to me."

Those incredible eyes looked highly amused again. She wondered what entertained him so much.

He rose to his feet and walked to the backpack, opening it. He palmed a small device in his hand, walked back to her, then sat down cross-legged on the bedding and showed her the small object. It was the size of a pack of cigarettes, all black, with a few buttons on it.

She frowned as she wondered what it was. She'd never seen anything like it.

He pushed a button and growled, staring at her, watching every move Casey made as she looked at the small box on his palm.

Something growled back from it.

Startled, she laughed. It had to be a mini recorder of some kind. She'd seen some of them before but none like the one he held. He pushed the button and growled again, released the button, and once more the box growled back.

Casey smiled at him. Obviously he liked toys. "I can buy you some way better ones than that. Wait until I get you hooked on music."

Biting his lip, he slowly stood again and walked to the edge of the cave, peering out at the thick curtain of water falling to the river below.

Casey watched, hoping that he was debating the idea of living with her. She didn't want him to live as he was.

She wanted to keep him.

Instant guilt ate at her for the thought. He wasn't a stray pet that she could take home and put a collar on.

Her gaze ran down his muscular, sexy body...

No, he definitely wasn't a pet. She wanted to keep him but it wasn't in a put-a-collar-on-him way. Not unless that collar came with some handcuffs to tie him to her bed, so she could lick his entire body during some fun sex games.

He walked to the backpack again and this time withdrew dry clothes. The material was like that of his other outfit, some sort of black leather. She remembered how the previous clothes fit him to a T—

A thought struck.

Someone had *made* those clothes for him.

Her heart squeezed in her chest. Was there another woman like Casey out there? Someone who'd made him clothes? Did he make a habit of saving strange women in the woods and making love to them? Is that how he got the toy and the outfits?

If that was the case, why wasn't he still with one of them?

Casey instinctively knew she wouldn't let him go so easily if she managed to get him home. She'd want to keep him for as long as she could.

After dressing, he put on his wet boots again. His eyes finally returned to her after he'd removed another set of clothes. He walked toward her, holding out the shirt and pants.

She hesitated before climbing to her feet. Running her fingers over the leather-like material briefly, she grabbed them and he backed up a few feet.

"I don't think these will fit me but at least they're dry. Thank you. They're cool. I've never felt or seen material quite like this. It looks like leather but it's softer."

He was grinning at her again. Giving him her back, she dropped the pants on his bedding to try to figure out the shirt. She put it on then discovered Velcro-like fasteners instead of buttons on the inside seam down the front. The garment was huge, but at least she didn't have to worry about anyone seeing her bra-free breasts flopping around under his shirt. It was that baggy. She had to roll the sleeves several times to find her hands.

As she bent over, he growled from behind her. She smiled as she turned her head. He was staring at her ass peeking out from the bottom of the shirt.

"An ass man, huh? I thought you wanted me to get dressed?"

He tore his eyes away from her exposed curves and nodded.

Bummer. The idea of doing it doggy style with him turned her on. She bet he was good at that...

Subtle guilt ate at her again. Just because he had some animal-like features didn't mean he liked to fuck like one.

She opened the pants and stepped into them. They were way too long for her body when she pulled them up all the way. His legs obviously went on for miles, judging by the extra material pooled at her feet. When she tried to fasten the pants, she discovered another dilemma when they sagged down to her hips, one wiggle from falling off. She rolled the pant legs at her ankles to avoid stepping on the bottoms, then held the waist up with her hand, as she contemplated what how to keep the pants up.

He was there, crouched in front of her before she saw him coming. He bit his lip, showing his sharp teeth as he studied the problem, then he rolled the top of the waist down a few times so it thickened around her hips and stayed in place.

He checked his handiwork before lifting his head, trapping her gaze with his.

Chapter Three

For the first time in her life, Casey felt like a sex addict. Naughty thoughts inundated her mind as she stared into his incredibly blue eyes. His masculine scent teased her nose. Just being near him made her hot, made her yearn for him to strip her naked again to repeat what they'd done together on his bedding.

She saw his nostrils flare as he sniffed at her, his eyes growing hungry when he stared at the V of her thighs. It was clear he could scent her arousal. His hands released her though, leaving her hips as he stood. He grabbed the backpack, shutting it, and hooked it over his shoulder as he moved back to her.

It almost dazed her how tall he was as she tilted her chin back to look at him. When both of them were lying down, he hadn't seemed a good foot taller than she was. She felt tiny compared to the big-boned, muscular male. Sexual attraction sparked between them like electricity. His lips parted as he softly growled at her in that sexy way of his.

"I don't know why, but *damn* do you turn me on."

She flushed when she realized she'd said that out loud.

He grinned, reaching out to cup her face with his hand. The man had great hands. Rough skin brushed her cheek. She almost turned her head to look at his palm but that meant she would have had to tear her eyes away from his, and she just couldn't do it. He nodded his head.

"I turn you on too?"

Blue eyes narrowed as he softly growled. Thick lips parted, showing his sharp teeth. A sigh came out next. Tearing his gaze away from her, he turned his head to stare behind them at the falling water for long moments. His body tensed when he looked back down at her, pointing to the water.

"You want us to leave? But we just got dressed. We'll get wet again, and those men are probably still looking for us right now. We should wait. If they find *me*, it's one thing. But nobody should get a good look at you. You know what will happen if someone sees you, don't you? They'll take one glance and know you're different. They'll—"

A growl cut her off. He shook his head, the hunger in his eyes replaced with anger.

Casey bit her lip. Had he been captured before? Was that why he looked furious? Had someone hurt him? She *really* wished they could talk to each other.

He took a deep breath, letting his touch fall away from her cheek. Then his fingers brushed down her arm to grip her hand and he turned, tugging her gently toward the water.

"No." She dug in her heels while yanking on his hand. "We need to stay here, where it's safe. At least for a little longer."

He turned quickly to face her and in the next instant, her world turned upside down for the second time today as her hip hit his wide shoulder. He was carrying her again, his arm locked behind the back of her knees to make sure she stayed put.

"Damn it! Put me down. You don't understand that when you attacked those two assholes, they would have called for backup. More people are out there looking for us, searching my property, and if we go out there right now, they *will* find us. But no one knows about this cave so we can hide out here until it's safe. We should stay hidden! We should—"

Casey gasped as the man just jumped from the ledge through the waterfall. Pounding icy water poured over her for a heartbeat before they were plunged into the river. She couldn't make a sound as her lungs seized in shock from the frigid cold. Her upper body floated on the water as he broke the surface, the arm still firmly locking her thighs to his chest. He was moving, swimming quickly for shore, and she felt the jar when his boots found purchase along the riverbed.

He strode out of the river quickly, running for the woods as if all one hundred and fifty pounds of her wasn't a burden. Using her hands, she shoved her long hair away from her face. There wasn't an inch of her not freezing from being drenched in river water. It was growing dark, so she knew they were only going to get colder as the night wore on.

Fear crept into Casey when he stopped to growl deeply, his body tensing over something he obviously saw or smelled. It was probably the state police, who would have been called in when the two deputies had been attacked. She knew for sure that's not how the police report would read, despite Big Foot actually saving *her* from the deputies. Now they were both going to be caught because he hadn't listened.

"Shit. What is it?" she whispered, in case they hadn't been spotted yet. "Take us back to the cave."

He growled deeper.

What petrified her was the fact that she heard another growl respond—that she instinctively knew hadn't come from the man carrying her.

It was close enough to let her know it came from something within easy range of them. She twisted, shoving frantically at the wet brown hair that fell over her face, trying to see around his wide back and failing. Were there two of them?

Did Big Foot have a brother?

Oh Crap—what if she was their new sex toy?

She didn't roll that way. If he expected to share her with another man, he was going to learn different real fast.

Or worse...what if they were enemies, like two bears crossing in the woods? Bears fought each other when they met up, unless they were the opposite sex and both in the mood for some loving. She'd heard bears fighting from home. It was rare that they ventured that close, but she knew the large beasts roamed her woods.

Shit—what if it *was* a bear?

The man holding her tightly was big, but he wasn't a match for a large, vicious animal.

Casey finally lifted and twisted enough to look behind her—and she spotted a second male who looked a *lot* like her Big Foot.

She stared opened-mouthed, upside down, at the new male who wore a similar leather-like outfit that matched the ones Casey and Big

Foot wore. His hair was long and wild, as well, but shades lighter than black. She saw glowing eyes, a different shade of blue, and they were focused on *her*. He growled deeper.

Casey's Big Foot growled back. It sounded like a threatening kind of growl that a predator used to warn off another animal. Fear filled her at the thought that they might fight.

Were her woods full of these things? Where the hell had they come from? She had a ton of questions but not a single answer. The man holding her took a deep breath, jerking his head at the other one and growling again. He wiggled his shoulder so the backpack hit the ground.

The second man tore his focus from Casey. He walked closer, grabbed up the backpack and stepped away, his head lowered, almost as if he was bowing, before he spun around.

Casey was finally shaken from her stunned silence when the male march deeper into the woods and Big Foot moved to follow him.

"Put me down."

To her annoyance, Big Foot ignored her. He kept walking, carrying her over his shoulder, so Casey was left to her meager struggles. She put her hands on the curve of his back where it met his firm ass, shoving upward, trying to lever herself so she wasn't dangling loosely. All it got her was a quick shift from Big Foot, her hip higher on his shoulder, making her center of gravity off so it was impossible to lift her upper chest away from his back.

It also brought her face closer to his ass, and she knew he'd done it on purpose.

She pushed again but finally gave up when she realized he wasn't going to put her down.

Casey's fear returned as they walked quickly through the woods. She was still shocked there were two of them, and she had no idea where they were taking her. What if there were more? What if they had a few dozen Big Foot men camping out on her land? Had she interrupted some annual Big Foot family reunion held secretly on her land? She fought a hysterical giggle at the thought.

The sun went down, the woods getting so dark that she couldn't see a thing anymore, but it didn't slow down either man. Casey, however, was starting to get a headache from all the blood settling in her head, and her still-damp clothes were getting colder in the dropping temperatures.

She sighed. "Big Foot guy?"

He softly growled at her, his hand rubbing her leg, but he didn't stop walking. They must have traveled for miles by now but his pace hadn't' slowed a bit.

"I'm getting a headache from this position. Do you understand? All the blood in my head is causing me pain."

Relief swept through Casey when he stopped. He shifted, letting her slide down his chest and adjusting her in his arms until they were almost nose to nose, which she could barely make out in the darkness. The moon hid behind dense trees overhead, making him just a dark shadow in a darker terrain.

Her hands gripped his shoulders as he held her effortlessly off the ground with one arm around her waist. With his free hand, he shifted her leg until she understood, clamped both of them around his hips and her arms around his neck. Two large hands cupped her ass and she locked her ankles together to help her hold on. She felt like they were being watched, but she wasn't sure if it was the other man or some wild animal.

"You can put me down. I can walk."

He released her butt with one hand and reached back to grip her bare foot, rubbing it. Casey nodded, understanding.

"Right. I don't have shoes. I've got to be heavy though. Isn't your back hurting? Your arms? Hell, the shoulder you've been lugging me on? I know you're big and strong, but geez."

He chuckled and then softly growled at her. He released her foot to cup her ass again, holding her firmly in front of him, nuzzling her cheek with his. Understanding what he wanted, she turned her head to let it rest against the warmth of his neck. She inhaled his wonderful scent, since her nose was touching his throat. Now that she wasn't blocking his view anymore, he started to walk again.

Casey relaxed in his arms, enjoying the feel of her Big Foot holding her. If he was determined to carry her, then she was going to let him. Blindly traipsing barefoot in the woods at night while she was cold and wet didn't hold any appeal. She shivered as the chilly wind blew through the trees and branches whispered above them. His body heat helped her stay warmer where she was pressed against him.

Before long, he stopped abruptly.

Casey's eyes flew open and she turned her head to see what he was looking at. It was too dark for her to see a thing—until light suddenly flared in the sky in the distance.

She frowned, studying the small light. Her eyebrows shot up. Was it a falling star?

Um...*no*.

She tried to wiggle out of Big Foot's arms when it became clear the flying light was streaking right toward them.

"Shit!" she whispered.

The hands on her ass squeezed gently. She turned her head to look at him, desperate for reassurance, but he was just a very dim shadow. A soft growl came from the other man and the mouth inches from hers responded.

Casey looked around again when she heard a slight engine sound.

What in the hell...?

Her jaw dropped open when her eyes found the streaking light again. It was *much* closer and it looked like some kind of plane—but it sure wasn't one she could identify.

She'd heard and seen plenty of helicopters in her lifetime. They weren't quiet. Even small planes didn't sound like this, and they all had blinking lights for use at night. And no way could even the smallest plane set down in a heavily wooded area that wasn't bisected by a long stretch of straight road. A pilot would have to be insane to even think of landing on any of the narrow country roads in *this* area. They were all too thickly laced with tunnels of trees that curved above them.

No. Not a plane. It was way too big anyway. This was something new.

Whatever it was, it hovered above them. She stared up in disbelief as some kind of door beneath it opened wide, until she was blinded by light. Forced to look away, she took in the area around them, bathed in that brightness. She could see they were in a small clearing in the trees, maybe twenty feet at its widest point.

Her gaze flew to her Big Foot and she clutched him tighter in terror.

His beautiful eyes sparkled while he studied her features. Releasing one side of her ass, he pointed up, a grin splitting his lips.

Casey shook her head. "You can't be serious. We aren't going in that thing, are we? What in the hell *is* it?"

He just continued to smile at her.

She startled when something dropped near them, would have actually leapt out of his arms to run away but his hold on her tightened. He recognized her fear but clearly wasn't concerned, if his smile was any indication.

Casey's shock turned to horror when she finally looked to her left and saw what had dropped from the craft.

"Hell no." She frantically shook her head. "No."

He was moving before she could even struggle further.

Her Big Foot gripped the harness-type contraption that dangled from the hovering vehicle above them. She doubled her efforts to make him put her down but it was useless. He growled at her, his amusement totally gone as he released the harness to grip her tightly in both arms.

Frantically shaking her head, she glanced from him to whatever that apparatus was. The lighted craft had to be a hundred feet above them. No way was she letting him strap her to that thing with some weird rope. Being arrested and possibly violated by her ex-boyfriend wasn't sounding so bad at that moment.

The other guy was suddenly there, strapping the harness on Big Foot since he wasn't letting her go. Those arms might as well have been steel bands locked around her waist. The other man had to shove his hands hard between Casey's body and the man gripping her, to secure the harness. The other man stepped back after the binding clicked into place—and then their bodies swung in the air as Big Foot's feet left the ground.

Instantly she stopped struggling. Or more accurately, she struggled in reverse, wrapping her arms around him tightly, gripping his waist with her legs. She clung to him, praying they wouldn't fall.

Wind battered them as they got closer to the bright light. Casey buried her face in Big Foot's neck. "Oh God. Don't drop me!" she yelled.

She could have sworn he chuckled.

His strong arms wrapped even tighter around her and she slammed her eyes shut, not wanting to look down. She knew he was brawny, but he *had* been carrying her for miles as they'd walked to this spot. She hoped now wasn't the time for him to tire.

The engine sound got louder. She braved opening her eyes when the wind died down, and saw they'd been lifted into a metal room, the source of the white light. She turned her head—

And stared in alarm at *another* Big Foot.

This one had wild red hair with glowing bright green eyes that fixed on her. He wore the same leathery, body-encasing outfit, making her think maybe it was some kind of uniform.

And every damn one of these guys was tall and muscular.

She had a really bad feeling that she'd been all wrong about Big Foot.

The mythical creatures were solitary, according to local legends—and they sure didn't have hovering aircraft.

Was he some kind of super soldier the government had created? Maybe a crazy scientist had made these men during some kind of secret, experimental Army project.

Who would ever volunteer to have their DNA changed? *She* sure as hell wouldn't. And if her guy was some secret Army person, why was he taking her back to his base?

More fear flooded her as they were lifted away from the open door to the metal floor. Big Foot touched the ground. His body relaxed but he still gripped her securely.

The redheaded man was as big as Casey's Big Foot. He looked at her with a friendly smile. Growling, he turned to the man holding Casey. Big Foot growled back with a wink. Casey had a really bad feeling as the redhead unhooked the tether from the harness and stepped back. Big

Foot turned then, still holding her, and moved for a closed metal door. As they reached it, he didn't have to touch a thing. The door obviously had some kind of motion sensor that activated, since it slid open automatically. Big Foot strode into a corridor.

"Put me down," Casey almost begged.

Big Foot kept walking until he turned down another corridor, completely ignoring her plea. He paused in front of one of many doors, releasing her with one arm to slap his palm on an electric pad on the wall. The door buzzed softly before sliding open. He walked inside, the door sliding shut behind them as soon as his body cleared it.

Casey twisted her head to frantically look around the room.

A big bed with built-in drawers under it took up most of the small space. Along one wall were shelves with more drawers. The walls were made out of some kind of shiny black metal material that was foreign to her, like so many things since laying eyes on Big Foot. There was an open door across the space that led to a bathroom, its large shower stall in plain view.

She was distracted from studying the room further when the arm wrapped around her waist shifted to lower her body from his hold.

As the man eased Casey to her feet, she stared up at him. He gazed back for a few seconds before turning away to walk to a small screen with buttons. It reminded her of some kind of weird-looking computer or small television. She saw him touch it with one finger, a bright blue screen coming on instantly, with weird symbols scrolling across the surface. He let his hand drop after pushing a few buttons and then turned back to Casey, his gaze on hers.

"Can you understand me now? This is a program running on the *conis* that should let us communicate easily."

Casey's mouth dropped open. She attempted words but nothing came out.

She'd seen his lips move, and she'd heard his soft growl, but *English words* had come out of speakers hidden somewhere in the room.

She tried to speak again. She didn't know what to think or what to say. Too many thoughts were streaming through her head.

Finally, something popped out of her mouth.

"You're not a Big Foot, are you?"

A black eyebrow arched. "I have big feet compared to *you*."

"Sasquatch. You're not one of them, are you?"

"I don't know what that is. I'm not familiar with different breeds of humans."

Humans?

She needed to sit down. Her mind was spinning hard.

He'd said that like "human" was a foreign word to him...and he had pronounced it wrong too. It came out "hum-ins". And his wording was strange. Different *breeds* of humans? They didn't have different breeds; they had different racial groups.

She took a few steps back to collapse on his bed so she didn't hit the floor, since her knees felt like they were turning to water. She never looked away from him.

A sigh escaped his lips. "You're surprised that I'm not human. What did you think I was? What is a Big Foot?"

"What *are* you?"

He hesitated. "I was told your Earth thinks life doesn't exist on other worlds. I hate to give you another shock…but that would be an incorrect theory. Because there *is* life out there. Much of it. I'm a warrior from the planet Zorn. We learned about your planet when a human woman was captured by another alien race, and held captive with some of our people.

"My people escaped their prison, and one of our Zorn warriors took that human as his bound. He is my brother. I believe you would be familiar with bounds as a term called 'marriage'. Some of my Zorn warriors came here to find human women to bound with. My brother and his human are very happy together."

Casey was really glad she was sitting as she stared at the tall, handsome *ALIEN*!

Her eyes flickered over the tight outfit hugging his body. No wonder he was so buff. It made sense if he was a warri—

Another thought struck. Were they some kind of warrior race here to attack Earth?

Her eyes widened. "Are you attacking my planet?"

A grin curved his lips. "No. Would you like me to?"

"No!"

He chuckled, reaching for the front of his outfit, starting to tug it open. "Good. War is something we don't back away from…but we don't start them either. We are an intelligent race. I apologize for not having an implant on me to insert into your ear so we could communicate immediately. I wasn't expecting you, Casey. I had gone down to the surface to get a look at your Earth. It is beautiful, and so different from my world. You only have one moon and it is so distant! Your wildlife is also very tame compared to those where I live. Is that why you are not a hunter or warrior race?"

She was clueless how to answer that last part. "You apparently never came across a bear," she finally said. "They're dangerous and huge."

"I did not." He opened his shirt to tear it off his body completely. He threw it at the open door to the bathroom area. "Remove your wet clothing. We'll shower. I am hungry. They will bring us something to eat. We have brought foods that the other human woman eats, the one who is bound to my brother. Since she likes them, I hope that you will as well."

She shook her head. "Back up."

He frowned but took a step back from her. Casey almost snorted.

"Not literally. It's a figure of speech. You're losing me. What implant? What do you mean, some of your men came here to find women? Aren't there any women on your planet? I'm so confused." She took a deep breath. "And what is your *name*? I've been calling you Big Foot but that was evidently way wrong."

He smiled. "My name is Argernon. My people call me Argis Argernon. Argis is my title and place on my planet. My father leads Zorn. I am second son in line to lead. But do not be intimidated by my place. My father is very healthy and so is my older brother Ral. I will never have to lead my planet.

"An implant is something I'll have you fitted with soon, but I don't want to do it here because it would be painful without a healer to insert it properly. We don't have one onboard currently. It is a small device that will be painlessly placed inside both of your ears. That way we don't need a *conis* to translate for us. You'll be able to understand me and any other Zorn who speaks."

He chuckled. "And there are many women on my planet. It's just that some men wanted bound to human women. My brother's bound has made quite an impression on a lot of our males."

"*Conis*?"

He pointed. "I think you would call that a computer. Is that correct? My brother's bound has been working with the translation programmer, so humans can instantly have a human frame of reference for some of our terms. It is still being tested but she taught me a few words, with their Zorn translations. She said they would be useful on Earth. Computer was one of them."

Casey bit her lip. "What other words did she teach you?"

He grinned. "Clit."

"What did you say?" She was sure she had to have heard him wrong.

"*Unis* is our word for clit." His smile spread wide as his eyes lowered to the V of her legs. "Our women have a *unis*. You call it a clit. That is the part of you that I—"

"I got it!" Casey flushed as she cut off the rest of that sentence. She remembered too well what he had done to her. "Okay. What other words did she give you to toss out there at humans?"

He cocked his head. "I think we'll discuss those words at a later time. I feel dirty and we are both wet with river water that doesn't smell good. Take off the clothing. Come with me to the shower. I will wash you and feed you."

"I have to go home soon."

He studied her. "I assure you that you will be returning home, Casey." He smiled slowly at her. "But first I want to get to know you. I want to get you out of those clothes."

She hesitated. He was an alien from another planet...but then, she'd made love to him before—twice—thinking he was a legendary creature.

She got up and undressed slowly. He might not be Big Foot, but he was still one sexy beast. She wanted a repeat of earlier. Her eyes devoured him as she continued to strip.

"Why did you make us get dressed, only to leave the cave and get wet again?"

He smiled. "It wasn't safe there. I called my ship to pick us up. You were cold. I wanted you here where you'd be more comfortable."

She supposed it made sense, in an alien way.

He watched her while removing his boots and pants. When they were both naked, she soaked in every wonderful exposed inch of him. Her attention fixed on his middle. Instantly her body responded to his thick arousal pointing right at her, showing her how horny he was. Her inner muscles quivered as moisture flooded between her thighs.

The bathroom was tiny. She eyed the toilet. It was fairly obvious what it was but it wasn't the same as the one at home. The shower captured her attention most. There weren't doors, or even a curtain separating it from the rest of the bathroom.

Argernon chuckled. "I apologize for the lack of amenities but this ship was designed as a jumper. Our women are not warriors, so we do not transport them on these ships. They weren't built with female comfort in mind. We couldn't bring one of our larger ships close to your Earth, out of concern that your planet's defenses would pick us up. When the jumper leaves orbit, we will meet up with our larger ship that waits for our return before going back to Zorn."

"A jumper?"

"A small craft designed for speed, to transport our warriors from one place to another within a shorter range. Usually this craft is used to transport our injured or to get us to battle quickly. There are only ten living quarters that are private, and one room that the crews shares, and it only has two decks. This is the largest living quarter on the jumper, which I took from the captain since I am Argis. I wanted more privacy afforded to me than is usually found on the jumper."

"And Argis means what?"

"I told you. My father leads Zorn. Argis is a title of my family. Argis is…" He paused, his mind working, before he shrugged. "It is my family status on our planet. My brothers and I are all Argis."

"Do you have sisters?"

"Yes."

"Are they Argis as well?"

He shook his head. "Bratha. That is their designation. It means the female of my family. My mother is Bratha Alluwn—Alluwn is her name. My sisters are—"

"I understand."

He grinned. "Do you understand how much I want you?" His gaze raked down her body.

Casey's body responded to the hunger glowing in his eyes. "Yes, Argernon."

Large, warm hands reached for her, gripping her waist as he lifted her over the edge of the shower stall. It just had a rim to keep the water from pouring out on the floor. Argernon made the water start by waving a hand in the air. He grinned when Casey gasped in surprise at the sudden soaking of warm water.

"Sorry I startled you."

The water came driving down like rain from above the entire space, instead of in a single stream, so she couldn't look up at him. She pushed her wet hair out of her face and lifted her hand to keep water from running into her eyes as she looked at his chest.

"How do you see?"

He chuckled. "They aren't meant for sharing. They are meant for cleaning up fast. We will wait to share our bodies until we get out. Just stand there to get unsoiled. The water will wash us with chemicals but do not swallow it or it will make you sick. It cleanses our skin and hair."

She let the water pour over her but moved closer to Argernon's body. He moved his hands on her hips, brushing his palms up and down her skin, until one hand left her to wave in the air, stopping the water. Casey wiped water away from her face in time to see Argernon toss his wet hair back. She stared up at his strong features, realizing just how handsome he was, even if he wasn't human.

As far as aliens went he was damn fine looking. Not that she had anything to compare him to.

"I want inside you now. Close your eyes and do not startle. You will feel heat."

He reached over to push on part of the shower wall. Casey heard a click and she shut her eyes. She gasped as hot air hit her from above and from three sides. It was like being in a wind tunnel of blasting heat. If someone hooked up fifty blow dryers in different locations it would be a close comparison. The water dried on her skin and the air blasts suddenly shut off. She opened her eyes to look at Argernon.

He was grinning. "It doesn't dry hair fully, but if you push the button enough it will. You do not want to do that though. It will make your skin dry and itchy." He reached for her again to brush his fingertips over her collarbones. "You are so pale and soft. Your skin is so delicate."

Biting her lip, Casey eyed him. "Are we going to talk or are you going to take me to your bed?"

A grin split his face. "Follow me." He let his hand slide to hers then he tugged at her to follow him out of the bathroom. "Let's go."

She followed him back to the sleeping area. It was a big bed—longer than a standard king-size bed but about as wide. A muscular arm hooked around her waist after Argernon suddenly spun to face her. She gasped as he jerked her off her feet, just tossing her so she landed on her back on the bed with a bounce.

"I saw a monitoring of one of my kind having sex with a human woman. Your sex is slightly different from women of my world. I want to learn everything about your body...and I want you to learn about mine. I am slightly different from your human men as well."

Excitement hit Casey. "Okay. I'm game."

He blinked and arched an eyebrow.

"'I'm game' is a slang term. It means 'I'm in' or 'I want to do that'."

He chuckled. "Good because we are doing a lot of it."

Chapter Four

Argernon climbed on the bed after Casey. He stretched out his six-foot-five body next to her. Casey rolled on her side to face him until just inches separated them. She let her eyes slowly scan down his body to take in every detail of his naturally tan skin. She wet her lips. Argernon was totally lickable in her book. She just couldn't decide where to start.

A soft growl came from his throat. "How am I different from your human men?"

"Your features are slightly different." She reached over to trace his nose with her fingertip lightly. "Definitely different here. You have sharp teeth and your lips are fuller. Your bone structure is stronger and more pronounced."

"Am I attractive to you? I find your nose to be attractive for such a small bump."

Casey laughed, nodding. He definitely was attractive to her. "My nose is a bump?"

"Definitely." His eyes went to her breasts. "I love your pale skin."

"Aren't any of your people this white?"

He shook his head. "Never. I like that your body is much softer to look upon than those of our women." His hand spread on her slightly rounded stomach as he rubbed her skin there. "You are very soft to touch as well."

Casey let her hand drift from his cheek, continuing slowly down to his chest, his stomach, to finally stop at his groin, her eyes following as she let her palm caress the head of his cock.

"You are bigger here than a human."

"In size? Aren't your men built like us? Am I thicker or longer than your men?"

She hesitated. "The head of your cock is larger than a human's. You're bigger everywhere than any man I've ever been with, but they were smaller guys, to be fair. Your tip is thicker, and you thicken again a few inches down, all the way to the base of your cock. It feels amazing."

That brought a grin from him. "That would explain how tight you are. You almost hurt me but it feels wonderful. You are perfect and feel incredible inside." His grin died as hunger made his eyelids droop. "You are softer inside than any Zorn woman I have ever taken."

"What's the difference?"

"You don't have rough ridges in your *voltia*. You are soft and the sensation..." He growled, moving closer. "I want you again. Your scent calls to me when you are aroused. I love how you taste. You flavor better, Casey. I inhale you when you want me and I have never been harder, or hurt more, to be inside a woman."

She had to remember to breathe. She guessed *voltia* was their word for vagina. Her nipples tightened, her pussy flooded with need; the memory of him between her thighs, when his tongue had stroked her clit, was a strong aphrodisiac. She couldn't wait any longer either. She wanted him now.

"Let's stop talking and get busy."

"Busy?" He rolled, suddenly pushing her on her back. "Does this mean you want me to fuck you?"

"Yes." She gripped his rock-hard cock between them, feeling him throb in her palm. Soft skin covered a steel-hard erection. "Please, Argernon. I want to feel you." She spread her legs wide as she tugged at him.

He didn't take any additional urging to settle his larger body into the cradle of her thighs. They stared at each other as he adjusted his hips, pressing his thick cock against her wet sex. He pushed slowly. Her body resisted the thick, blunt head at the first press against her but Casey just lifted her hips to take him, spreading her thighs more, opening herself wider to accept him. The sensation of him pushing into her, stretching her, made her moan in pleasure. It was pure bliss as he filled her, sliding against all those wonderful nerve endings.

"That feels so good. You feel like heaven." She paused. He probably didn't know what that term meant. "Nothing has ever felt better than you do inside me."

"Casey," he growled. "I am trying to refrain. Don't get me too turned on or I am afraid I'll hurt you."

That got her to grin. "Hurt me?"

He didn't smile back. "I am much stronger and I don't want to harm you."

An image of him fucking her hard and deep surfaced in her imagination. In the cave, he'd lost some of his restraint in the end, while they'd been going at it. It had been a heaven and hell that she wanted to experience again. Her inner walls gripped him tighter with need. She wanted him like that. Fast, hard, unrestrained and wild. His cock almost withdrew from her completely, causing more wonderful sensations. A moan tore from her.

"I think I can take it, Argernon." She wiggled her hips. "Give me what you've got."

A growl tore from Argernon's lips as he drove into her hard and deep.

The sudden thrust made her throw her head back in rapture, her fingernails digging into his shoulders as a loud moan tore from her lips.

Argernon froze, buried deep inside her. He started to slowly withdraw. "I am sorry I hurt you."

She shook her head, opening her eyes. Her legs wrapped around his waist to lock him in place. "That didn't hurt. It surprised me but it feels amazing. Do it again."

"Are you sure?" Concern showed in his gaze.

"I'm not fragile. Trust me."

He withdrew from her body, forcing her to release him from her legs. He pushed up to his knees to stare down at her.

"Roll over then and give me your ass."

"Wow." She swallowed. "Uh…I think you're way too big to go there."

He tilted his head, frowning at her. "I want to take you that way."

She blinked. "You're kind of thick for that. I'd be game but it would take some time to work you in, and we'd need lubrication." Her gaze flickered down to his impressive hard-on. "Lots of lube."

Argernon's frown deepened as confusion flicked across his features. "You're ready for me."

She bit her lip. "Are we both talking about anal sex? Do you know what that is?"

He shook his head. Surprise hit Casey. They didn't have anal sex on his planet? That was just weird. After a quick glance at his thick-headed cock, she couldn't say she was disappointed that he wasn't going to go there. He was too thick to do the anal thing without some pain involved. She slowly rolled over to get on her hands and knees. Turning her head, she smiled at him over her shoulder, wiggling her ass in invitation and pushing it up higher, since he was a tall guy even on his knees.

"Like this?"

"You make me so hard," he snarled at her.

He dropped down on her body, caging her under him as he braced one hand on the bed to hold his weight, his free hand guiding his cock. He pushed into her pussy slowly. Both of them groaned loudly as he worked himself in deep.

"You are so hot, so wet and tight."

"It feels really good from this side too," she moaned as he moved in short thrusts that teased her. Her fingers clawed his bed. "Please fuck me hard—and faster."

"My pleasure," he growled.

His free arm hooked around her waist, anchoring her so she couldn't move as he hammered her rapidly and deeply. His hand shifted, cupping her from the front as his palm rubbed against her clit. Flesh hit flesh as her ass slapped his groin. Casey couldn't think through the rapture she felt as his cock pounded relentlessly. Something wonderful was building, her muscles tensing as she hovered on total ecstasy.

"Oh God!" Casey panted. "Oh God! Don't stop."

"I couldn't if I tried," he snarled.

Sharp teeth gripped her shoulder. Another snarl tore from Argernon, muffled against her skin locked between his teeth, his hips powering into her even faster. Their bodies slammed together. Her vaginal walls clamped down tighter on his driving cock.

Casey screamed as she came hard. His teeth released the tight hold on her shoulder as Argernon threw his head back. A roar tore from his parted lips, his body quaking over hers fiercely, his hot semen blasting inside Casey while he emptied his release into her. His hips slowed until he wasn't moving anymore.

Casey collapsed her shoulders to the bed, her ass still in the air, since Argernon had his arm braced around her hips to hold her in place. She panted and fought the urge to pass out from exhaustion. The man had fucked her to within an inch of her life and she knew it. A smile twisted her lips. He was still planted inside her. His hand moved, his fingers exploring her clit. It made Casey jerk a little since her flesh was now oversensitive.

A chuckle sounded from him before he slowly withdrew, his fingers moving from her clit. Casey missed the feel of him inside her body. The arm holding her up gently slid away and Argernon collapsed onto his side. Casey let her ass lower as she stretched her legs straight out, until she was on her stomach on his comfortable bed. She rolled to her side so they faced each other.

"That was the best sex I've ever had in my life," she admitted with a grin. "You're amazing and I almost feel like thanking you."

Argernon grinned back. "It was the best for me as well, and I *do* thank you. You have made me very happy."

Casey chuckled. "So do you go around saving women from getting arrested often?"

He frowned. "Why were they arresting you? I am familiar with this term. On Zorn, it means you have broken laws and are taken to be judged for punishment if you are found guilty. I want you to tell me everything."

"I told you I dated the wrong guy who slept with another woman. Last week, those two deputies you rescued me from? He had them arrest me. They handcuffed me, took me to Don's office, and after they left, he…" She flushed a little. "He wanted me to be with him again. I told him off. He started pulling down my pants and said some really awful things to me. I fought and screamed. He was going to force me to have sex with him but he had to let me go when his deputies burst into the room. He sent them back today to arrest me again." She shivered. "This time he might not have been stopped. I ran but they caught me. That's when you found me. Thank you, Argernon."

70

Anger made his mouth twist into a tight frown, intense blue eyes burned with rage. "I can understand wanting to be inside you desperately but to force a woman is inexcusable. I have heard you are a monogamous species. He was aware of this? That being with another woman sexually would make you not want him anymore?"

His words stunned her. She swallowed. "Not all humans are monogamous, but most of us are—and yes, he was aware. I take it that your world doesn't practice monogamy?"

Dread of what his answer might be made her stomach clench. Not that it should matter to her, but the idea of him with another woman bothered Casey. He was from another *planet*. That whole "take him home with her" idea was already blown to hell. She knew she was going to lose him...she just didn't want to.

Depression hit her hard. She wished he *had* been a Big Foot in need of a home. It wasn't like they could enter into a lasting relationship now. Of course he'd go back to his home planet.

"My world is different. Our males are highly aroused often. Do you understand what I say?"

"It means you have a high sex drive."

Argernon nodded. "Our women can't handle one of our men alone. Most men have two or three women in his home under his protection. We only bound with one woman. She is the one we favor the most, and share our seed with to have offspring."

Casey had to shut her mouth since it had fallen open. She didn't like what he was saying and reminded herself it was a good thing they weren't in a long-term relationship, no matter how much something inside her rebelled at that thought.

"How many times a day do you have sex?"

He shrugged. "Perhaps five times a day, every day."

That was a high number but nothing Casey couldn't handle. Hell, the guy was amazing in bed. "Why can't your women handle that?"

"Our women are different than you physically. I have read the medical reports that were collected on my brother's bound, and she has the ability to enjoy sex many times in a day. Our women get sore and usually do not enjoy the sex more than two times in a day. Their *unis* swells and is uncomfortable after sex. Their *unis* is inside their bodies and not on the outside, like your clit is."

"Wow." Casey let the information sink in.

"That is one of the reasons so many of our men wish to bound with a human female. Not only can you match us for sexual desire, but you enjoy sex in many positions that are not enjoyable to our women. What they do not yet know is how wonderful it feels to touch you, how different you are inside, and by the Lord of the Moons, you feel *amazing*."

Casey smiled at him. She reached out to let her fingertips explore his muscled chest. "That goes both ways."

His eyes narrowed. "You are aroused again, aren't you?" His nostrils flared. "I want you so much I hurt for you. Can I take you now?"

Lowering her eyes, Casey was amazed that Argernon was hard again. She ran her hand down his body to grip his hard shaft near the base, gliding her palm upward to the larger mushroomed tip. She brushed her thumb around the rim of the tip in a slow circle. Argernon softly groaned as he rolled on his back.

"Please touch me, Casey. Your hands are soft and pleasure me greatly."

Casey straddled Argernon's thighs. She used both hands to explore his balls, testing their heavy weight, and taking notice of the fact that there was almost no hair there. She released him with one hand, sliding it up his shaft toward the thick tip.

A hard, nickel-sized patch of skin sat on the top of his cock, slightly ridged along the upper half. Argernon whimpered when her fingers explored it. His large body jerked under hers.

Casey froze. Her gaze flew up to his face.

"Did I hurt you?"

He shook his head. "That's my *hais*. Feel the harder area? I would compare it to your clit, from the way you react to me touching you. It is the most sensitive area on my cock."

Casey ran her fingers over him, exploring every glorious inch of Argernon. He shivered under her soft touches as she cupped his balls with one hand and rubbed the palm of the other over his head. He had little pubic hair but lots of chest hair that trailed down his front to his waist.

Argernon shivered again. "I need inside you. I can't take the teasing." The words came out in a raspy tone.

Casey was thrown onto her back in a heartbeat when he sat up. She gasped as his body came down on her smaller one. He pinned her, using his knees to spread her thighs wide open, and entered her without warning. Casey moaned, gripping his shoulders, wrapping her legs around his hips, and pulled him tighter against her. He stretched her inner walls with his thickness, filling her in one slow drive of his hips.

She cried out in bliss. "You feel so good."

Argernon rode her hard and fast. He shifted the position of his hips, lifting her body higher by wrapping an arm under her ass to elevate her. He braced his other arm on the bed to lift his upper body off her chest. Her hands instead ended up gripping his driving hips.

If it were at all possible, Argernon moved faster and harder, pounding into her over and over.

Casey came furiously, pleasure exploding as his hips slowed. He groaned as his cock pulsed strongly against her vaginal walls, semen flooding her as he came. Opening her eyes, she watched Argernon's face. He almost looked like he was in pain, his mouth open to show off his Zorn fangs. His beautiful blue eyes were squeezed shut and his head thrown back. The pained look eventually passed to one of peace when his eyes slowly opened.

A smile touched her lips. "That was…" She was no longer sure what words could cover the amazing experience of having sex with Argernon.

"I know."

Casey caught her breath. She was getting too attached to this man, and she knew it. She hesitated before asking, "Why did you bring me here?"

Slowly withdrawing from her body, his eyes looked anywhere but at her.

His features hardened, all emotion wiped from his face. He moved away from her to stretch out on his back next to her on the bed...then turned his head and finally met her eyes.

"I don't understand the question."

Casey rolled to her side, facing him. She hadn't missed his reaction to her question. "Why did you really take me from the cave and bring me here to your ship? You were staying there. I saw your sleeping bag. It wasn't that cold. Why return to your ship now?"

He hesitated. "I didn't want our time to end."

She didn't want it to either. She swallowed. "I have to go back in two days, Argernon. I don't work until then, but the day after tomorrow, I have to be back at noon. That's twelve o'clock during the day, Earth time." She suddenly laughed. "Earth time. Boy, does that sound funny to say. I'm still trying to come to grips with the fact that I'm on a ship of some sort, and that you're not from Earth. How weird is that?"

He didn't smile back. Instead his blue eyes narrowed and seemed to harden. "We need to talk about that, Casey."

"We *are* talking."

He hesitated before lying on his side and reaching for her. One of his hands cupped her hip, his large, warm fingers curled around her hipbone to grip her firmly. "I'm not taking you back."

He said the words softly.

Casey let his words sink in. "Excuse me? What did you say?"

He sighed. Bright blue eyes glowed at her with intensity. "I'm not taking you back. You know about us. The moment I heard you running through the woods, I made a choice to save you. Those men didn't really see me well. You thought I was a Big Foot. But now you know the truth—that I am not something that can be explained away. My men want to find women on your planet, and we can't do that if your people are aware of our existence or our visits. We aren't looking for a war and we don't want to fight with your people, but we do want some of your women to bound with. I am not taking you back."

Shock hit Casey hard before anger flared. "You have to take me back. As much as I've enjoyed this..." She waved a hand between them. "I own my home, have a job, and friends. Not many friends, I admit, but I have a life and it's *mine*. You have to take me back, Argernon!"

He took a deep breath, letting it out slowly. "I wasn't looking for a woman to bound with and I hadn't even considered it until I met you. I didn't pull out of you at the end of sex. I planted my seed in you, Casey. I bound to you. You are mine now, and I'm taking you back to Zorn with me. I will do my best to make your life happy. You will enjoy Zorn. It is a beautiful planet. My brother's bound is human and she loves living there.

She is happy—and you will be too. I will commit to making sure you are content."

Casey was too astonished to speak for long moments. He was taking her to another planet? Was it even in the same galaxy? He doubted that mattered; he looked dead serious, judging from the stern expression on his face.

She'd wanted to take him home to keep him. Now he was taking *her* home to keep instead.

Rolling away, she jerked out of his hold and got to her feet. She paced his small room, shaking her head wildly. She glared at Argernon when she stopped walking.

"No way in hell. You have to take me home. You can't just adopt me and take me home like I'm some pet! You can't take me from my planet. It's kidnapping and I won't go!"

Argernon flinched. He slowly climbed off the bed as well. He kept a good four feet between them. Regret shone in his eyes. "I am sorry, Casey, but I bound you. The sex was too intense and I did not expect my overriding desire, or the fact that I would not be able to bring myself to pull out of you. There's something else I should tell you."

"I am going home, Argernon," she said softly, firmly. "You can't keep me here."

He blinked a few times. "I *can* keep you, and I will. You could be carrying my offspring, Casey. We are breeding compatible." His gaze lowered to her stomach. "Even now my seed could be taking root." He looked into her eyes. "I am only sorry that you are so distressed to stay with me. I was hoping you would be pleased."

"Pleased?" She gaped at him. "You're kidnapping me from my life, Argernon! From everything I know! I have a home and a job."

He took another deep breath. "Now you will have a new home that you will share with me. Your job will be as my bound. I will cherish you and protect you. I will feed you and care for you. That is your new life."

"You son of a bitch!"

Argernon frowned. "I don't understand. In my language, a bitch is a female animal in mating drive."

"Exactly!"

His lips twisted into a grimace. "My mother—" He closed his mouth. "Insults are your human way of dealing with anger. I understand. It doesn't change anything. I am sorry you are upset. I was hoping for your happiness—but I *will* keep you."

Chapter Five

Casey was locked in Argernon's room and she was considering committing murder. He had dressed himself, and given her a large shirt to wear. He'd brought her some kind of fruit plate with pieces of cooked meat. She had no idea what kind of meat it was but it wasn't like anything she'd ever tasted before. It was some kind of long strip of steak that was tangy and delicious. The fruits had been terrific as well, if not strange looking. The drink he'd given her was red, its taste similar to fruity-flavored water.

But before she'd even eaten a bite, he'd left her alone to brood—hours ago.

She'd tried to get the door open but it wouldn't budge. She only had access to his room and to the bathroom. In her search of both, however, she *had* found a super-sharp weapon that looked like a cross between a dagger and a pair of scissors, which was now stashed under the pillow on the bed.

Rage boiled inside her as she paced. Argernon couldn't kidnap her to take her to another planet. So she'd had sex with the guy? Admittedly, it had been great sex, but that didn't mean he could keep her like a pet. Sitting down hard on the bed, she tossed her wet hair over her shoulder. She'd figured out the shower, and since she was furious with him, she didn't want to smell like Argernon or sex, so she'd washed all traces of him off her body.

He'd left her because he said he had duties to perform. What in the hell did that even mean? What did the guy do besides going around having sex with strangers and kidnapping them after the fact?

Casey continued to burn with fury that she refused to let go of—because if she let it go, she knew the fear would grip her.

The thought of being taken to another planet, where she'd be at an alien's mercy, terrified her. She didn't know Argernon at all besides how amazing he was at fucking her. For all she knew, he could be abusive. Hell, she thought she'd known her ex-boyfriend Don way better, and he'd turned out to be a cheating bastard, a liar, and in the end, had used his job to almost rape her. What horrible character traits was Argernon hiding that she'd discover down the road?

The fact that he was a kidnapper was already pretty clear.

The door slid open suddenly, startling Casey. She glared at the tall alien as he entered the room. Argernon studied her as he paused inside the door that shut firmly behind him—the door that seemed to work just fine for him. Obviously the pad wouldn't open for just any handprint. Argernon glanced around the room before his attention returned to her.

"How many weapons did you find?"

Casey swallowed hard. "None. I wish I'd thought of that."

Snorting, Argernon edged around the room, keeping his distance, but he watched her closely as he moved. "I assume that an intelligent, angry female of *any* race is spiteful, Casey. Hand over the weapons that you found. If you harm me, it won't do you any good. There are over a dozen men on this ship that will not let you leave. We have left your planet's orbit and have docked with our ship. There is nowhere to escape to."

"You're lying to me."

"I do not lie. It is a useless endeavor and not honorable."

"So kidnapping a woman is honorable?"

He frowned. "I did not plan on this, Casey. I went to your woods to visit your Earth and seek out your wildlife. I'm a hunter by nature and I wished to explore. I never counted on seeing you running from those men or saving you."

"You took me to the cave. You planned *that*."

"I wanted you, yes, but that was after I had rescued you. You drew me. You still draw me. I want you right now. No woman has ever made me feel as you do. I can't resist you."

Casey's gaze flew to the front of his tight black pants. He was clearly turned on. The outline of his thick cock was unmistakable. He was definitely not lying about wanting her. She jerked her gaze up to his face to glare some more.

"Too bad for you I'm not some brainless slut who sees a big dick and forgets everything just to fuck a man. Let me go, Argernon. I want to go back. It's been fun—well, up until you told me I couldn't go home. I'm not a pet you can leash and adopt. I'm a person and I have a *life*."

"Hand over the weapons you found in my quarters."

Glaring harder, she stood up to move around the bed so it was between them. "I don't know what you're talking about. I'm not a warrior.

I'm a woman. Let me go home, Argernon!" She decided to change tactics. She softened her voice. She wasn't above a little begging. "Please?"

He arched an eyebrow. "And what if you are carrying my offspring? Our seed is very aggressive. That is why, on my planet, we only give our seed to our bound. Controlling who we have offspring with is impossible otherwise. Every time one of our scientists came up with a form of medication that prevented fertilization, our seed overcame it. We are a very virile race. Zorn seed has already taken root in a human woman. My brother brought life to the human womb of his bound."

"If you knew this, then why the hell didn't you pull out?" Casey scowled. "Oh hell, that doesn't work sometimes anyway, does it? Women get pregnant all the time that way."

"Pulling out before our seed spills does work with Zorn. Only our seed after climax is viable for producing offspring."

"Then why didn't you pull out of me?!"

He was frowning. Argernon sighed as he let his arms drop to his sides. His hands brushed his thighs, rubbing them nervously.

Finally, his intense blue gaze locked with Casey's. "I was unable to resist. I seem to have little to no control when I am inside you." He paused. "You are…an anomaly. I planned to seduce you and not spill my seed inside you. I just couldn't resist. It's why we left the cave and came to the ship. You could be carrying my offspring. It changed everything."

"Look who's talking," she muttered. "Fine. You're obviously an advanced race. You flew this ship here. You have all kinds of shit I can't even identify in this room. You're more highly developed in technology than my people are, so give me a test and if I'm *not* knocked up, then let me go."

He frowned. "Your terms are...strange. I think I followed what you said. I do not want to give you up. I am keeping you if my seed took root inside you or not. I bound you, Casey. I did learn one Earth saying from my brother's bound." Bright blue eyes narrowed. "Deal with it."

"You son of a bitch!" She wanted to slap him.

"I must admit to you that your insults do not produce their intended result. I do not feel offended by that remark which you have used twice now."

"Fuck you."

He grinned suddenly. "With pleasure." He reached for the front of his pants.

"No! That's not what I meant. It wasn't an offer or a request. It... Oh hell." Casey was furious. "Keep your pants up. No way am I letting you touch me again. 'Fuck you' said in anger is an *insult*. It means something bad, you big alien jerk."

Argernon's fingers froze on his pants. He softly growled at her. "I want you and you want me. I understand that you are infuriated, and I even understand that you feel I have somehow betrayed a trust by keeping you. It doesn't change the fact that I have bound you and you are mine now, Casey. I am taking you home with me. You will like it. We can fight about this but in the end, the result will be the same. You will live in my home as my bound."

"You have to sleep sometime, Argernon."

He tilted his head slightly. "Everyone sleeps. What do you mean by that wording?"

She glared at him. "It means if you want to live a long life, you'll rethink this and take me back home. It means you can't be on your guard all the time—and when you are sleeping, you are vulnerable. You might be stronger than me, but I'm not completely helpless."

Rage hit his features. "You are threatening to kill me?"

"Shit," Casey muttered as fear filled her. The guy was enormous and a warrior. He was incredibly strong and she wasn't likely to ever forget it, since he'd carried her for miles as if she weighed nothing. "Just let me go," she said softly. "*Please.*"

He moved lightning fast. Casey saw him coming in the blink of an eye but had nowhere to go. She screamed when he grabbed her arms, then her feet left the floor before she flew through the air and hit the bed facedown, hard. She expected pain but there was none—even when her hands were yanked behind her back.

One of his hands restrained her wrists together. Casey heard material tear. She thrashed but couldn't see what he was doing with her hair in the way. She shook her head, trying to clear the long strands away from her eyes.

"Let me go!" She tried to turn over but a knee came down on her ass, also without pain. He only applied enough weight on her backside to hold her pinned tight to his bed. "Damn it! Get off me!"

Material was wound around her wrists. She continued to struggle but she couldn't get free. She did manage to turn her head to see that he'd somehow torn a strip from the sheets, which he was now using to tie her wrists. His hand released her when he finished but the material held her wrists together. He removed his knee to step away from the bed.

"Let me go, damn you!" She rolled on her side, struggling to her knees.

Argernon growled at her. He gripped the front of her shirt at the neckline, giving it a hard yank. Material tore all the way open along the front of the shirt so Casey's chest and stomach were exposed. Casey gasped as she dove for the bed. She was back on her stomach, but at least her breasts were covered. Throwing her head back to clear hair out of the way, she glared at him over her shoulder.

"If you force me, I *will* kill you, you son of a bitch!"

Argernon eyed the room before his attention returned to the bed. A growl tore from his throat. The translator was malfunctioning, Casey thought, or maybe there weren't words for the angry sounds he was making. He tore the top blanket from the unmade bed, yanking it from beneath her and sending the pillows flying.

His dagger-scissors thing went flying with them, hitting the floor. Argernon's outraged gaze moved from the dagger to her.

"No weapon, Casey? What is that?"

"I have no idea *exactly* what that is. It's not like anything I've seen before. It was in *your* bathroom, you tell *me* what the hell it is."

He growled again, storming for the fallen sharp object. He yanked it up, stomped to the door, and slammed his hand on the sensor to open it. Casey watched with dread as he threw her only weapon somewhere

85

down the corridor. She saw a man stop to stare curiously into the room. Another Zorn warrior, one she'd never seen before. He had jet black hair, tan skin, was as big as Argernon, and wearing almost the same black outfit.

The man's eyes terrified Casey as she stared back at him. They were totally black, giving them an evil appearance.

Argernon snarled at the man in the corridor. "Keep walking, Daros."

The man tore his stare from Casey to smirk at Argernon. "Are you having problems with your human? Need a hand? I'm good at seducing women."

Argernon roared before he stepped back. The door slammed shut, blocking the curious gaze of the black-eyed Daros, who was left standing in the corridor. Argernon turned and snarled in fury.

"Is that what you want? Should I hand you over to another male, since you find me so distasteful that you wish to kill me with my own *shara*?"

"I don't know what a *shara* is, and don't you dare let someone else touch me!" Terror rolled through her at the thought of Argernon letting another man near her. Tears filled her eyes. "Please don't let someone hurt me."

He took some ragged breaths. "A *shara* is used to cut hair when it gets too long, and it is also a good weapon to keep nearby in case of attack. And I didn't mean that about another male. I am furious, Casey, but you are my bound. I will kill any man who touches you. If your human men share their women, then I am as unlike a human as a man can get. Are we understanding of each other?"

Relief hit her. "Yes."

"Good." He started to remove his clothing. He still looked pissed. "Stop looking at me like that."

"Why are you taking off your clothes?" Fear and anger were trading places again. "Stop getting naked."

"It is impossible to make you want me while both of us are dressed. Our clothing would only get in the way."

Casey had a really bad feeling. "You're going to force yourself on me?"

Argernon shot her another angry look. "Never. Harming is the last thing I would do to you, Casey. I never want to bring you pain." His amazing eyes narrowed, his thick lips tightening into almost a smirk. "I feel confident that I can make you want me."

"Oh shit," Casey muttered.

She was certain he could make her want him too, if he really put his mind to it. Hell, if he put half his mind to it. They already knew their sex was combustible. Rage and fear continued their battle for dominance. She felt as if she were on an emotionally charged rollercoaster ride. She just wanted off—and not in the sexual way that Argernon was obviously set on.

She watched him with dread as he stripped completely. She visually inspected his perfectly tan body. Just looking at Argernon, with all those ridged muscles and that sexy long hair, made Casey want him.

In seconds, she had one very turned-on, sexy, hot alien standing at the end of the bed. His gaze roamed her backside before he very slowly bent over her.

"I won't forgive you if you seduce me," she said softly. "I'm angry and I don't want you. That should be enough for you to respect my feelings, to not do this."

Argernon had the nerve to chuckle. "Do your Earth men believe it when human women say these things?"

Casey shot him a glare over her shoulder. Her neck was starting to hurt from twisting her head to see him. "Yes, they do."

His eyes sparkled with amusement. "You are making me think your males aren't smart if they can't handle an angry woman." He gripped the back of the damaged shirt still clinging to her body and shredded it, doing whatever it took to remove it without untying her wrists. He tossed the pieces over his shoulder to the floor.

She tried to roll away but Argernon gripped her hips with both of his large hands to yank them up, forcing her to her knees. With her hands tied behind her back, she couldn't brace her upper body. Her head and chest were against the bed with her ass up high in the air, where he held her in place.

"Stay like this."

"Go to hell, Argernon. You kidnapped me. You won't let me go home. I don't want you seducing me."

His roughened, calloused palms caressed her skin. A shiver ran through her when he captured her ass with both hands, gripping her firmly. One finger slid along the line of her slit between her thighs, that same finger finding her clit. He tapped the sensitive nub repeatedly. His other hand shifted its hold on her butt, the thumb finding her pussy entrance, to rub back and forth a fraction inside her.

Casey squeezed her eyes shut. Her body responded to the large Zorn, no matter what her mind wanted.

He bent over her farther, his large frame pressed against her curved body. Argernon's long hair teased where it fell against her naked back. Hot breath fanned her skin when moved in closer to her neck. His lips hesitated just next to her ear.

"You are mine now, Casey. I won't let you go. I can't. We're bound together. You can't deny what is between us. Do you think I could return to my planet and just forget you? Could you truly forget about me?"

She hated the fact that he was right. She could never forget Argernon. They were too damn good together. If he were human and wanted to live on Earth, she'd be moving him into her house just to keep him in her bed permanently.

But he wasn't human, and he was taking her to his home world.

"Let me go, Argernon. Return me to Earth. You can't just take me away from everything that I know and expect me to be happy about it."

He nipped her shoulder lightly with his sharp teeth. "*I am all that you will know. I will be everything to you, as you are now everything to me. I will never release you or return you to your planet. I will make you as addicted to my body as I am to yours. You belong to me, Beautiful.*" His thick thumb worked inside her a little deeper, finding the evidence of her response to him, and using the wetness to slowly fuck her with shallow movements. "I will teach you that we belong together, Casey. Agree to be my bound."

Casey bit back a moan. She shook her head against his bed. If she gave in to him, she'd be giving up her life on Earth. She'd never see her home again. She'd end up on some strange planet facing complete uncertainty.

She tensed as his hands and mouth continued to tease her. Her mind might be rebelling but her body was on Argernon's side of the argument. His thumb moved deeper, sliding in and out of her with ease in slow, teasing motions as her body got wetter with need.

"No. I want to go back to Earth. You can't just go around kidnapping women."

Argernon's movements ceased. He slowly lifted his body away from hers and growled softly at her. "I'm a warrior, Casey. I never back away from a fight. I will never give you up."

"Go fuck yourself!"

"I don't want to find self-release. You showered while I was gone. I don't smell myself on you. You did this on purpose, didn't you?"

Casey decided to plead the Fifth and she didn't say a word. She couldn't see him anymore, now that he had her ass in the air. She heard the Zorn sniffing at her before he groaned softly. The thumb jerked out of her pussy, his other hand moving away so he couldn't reach her clit anymore. He gripped her hip to keep her in place.

"You definitely washed my scent off you on purpose. You even cleaned inside. You are getting wet, I smell your arousal, but my seed does not scent on you. I can't taste it either." He growled. "I don't like that. You are *mine*, and I like you scenting of my seed and sex."

"And I want you to take me back home to my planet," she ground out. "Isn't life a bitch when you don't get what you want?"

He softly growled. The translator stayed silent. She guessed that was just more angry sounds. Panic flashed briefly in Casey. He said he'd never harm her physically, but she was still helpless and vulnerable in this position. "Don't hurt me, Argernon."

"I am debating on your punishment. If you were a Zorn woman, I would spank you first then tease your body, refusing to allow you to climax until you begged me. That is how they learn a lesson. Do your Earth men spank their willful females?"

"Please don't do that."

"I assume they do not. Your skin is so soft it might cause you real pain." One of his hands released her hip to cup her ass firmly. His other hand rubbed the back of her thigh. "I would never hurt you, Beautiful. You want me. You are highly aroused. Is it the thought of punishment, being tied down, or the memory of my body joined with yours that makes you want me?"

"Go to hell."

"I don't know this place but I am sure it is not good, judging by your tone." He lowered his face until his long hair brushed her body again. He inhaled. A growl tore from deep in his throat, rumbling in his chest. "You smell so needy for me. You call to my body."

He released her, moving away, and Casey rolled on her side, watching Argernon as he walked to the storage wall. He bent, rummaging in a drawer before turning around.

His cock was jutting straight out to rise thickly, proving that he was really turned-on. But she quickly tore her eyes from his hard-on—because what he held in his hand got her full attention.

Her mouth dropped open as Argernon returned to the bed and brandished the item he'd retrieved—two wrist restraints made out of thick leather, with a short chain binding them together.

"Please," she said softly. "I wouldn't have used that knife thing on you. That's why it was hidden in the bed and not on my body. I'm not a warrior. I don't even know how to fight. I was pissed off, um...mad at you. Please, Argernon. Don't do anything bad to me."

He grinned, showing teeth. "You do not believe me when I say I will not hurt you? We use sexual frustration on Zorn to punish our women and make them submit."

"That doesn't look painless. What are you going to do with those? With me?"

He leaned over, his glowing blue eyes narrowing. "Anything I want, Beautiful. I will teach you that you belong to me. You are my bound. I give you my seed. I give you my home to share, and my protection. I will feed you, care for you, and make you happy, even if I have to teach you appreciation. You will be taught to not fight me—and you *will* bend to my will."

Casey glared at him. "I won't be broken."

"I don't want you broken. I want you to want me as much as I want you."

Argernon grabbed her and pushed her flat on her stomach again. A knee went on her ass to painlessly pin her down. The chains rattled when the restraints hit the bedding next to her. He untied her hands but gripped them in one of his own as he put a restraint on her left wrist.

He releasing her briefly and she swiftly rolled, trying to punch him with her free hand.

A large hand enclosed her fist, catching it before she even got close to hitting him. He gently forced her arm to her chest and shackled the other wrist into the restraint, this time with an amused expression on his face. The restraints were surprisingly comfortable, padded with something soft.

She was shackled in front now—a small mercy—with about a foot of chain between her wrists. Argernon grabbed it in the middle. Backing up, he straightened from the bed, pulling her up by the chain.

Once she was standing, Casey kicked at Argernon.

He avoided her bare foot with a laugh. With a jerk, her arms were lifted over her head, high enough to put her on her tiptoes. He kept her stretched up while he smiled down at her.

"You are willful, Casey. I like that."

"Just wait. I'll show you willful, asshole. How's that for an insult? Do you know what an asshole is?"

Eyes narrowed as his smile faded. "I do. I am not an asshole."

"It depends on who you ask. Let me go, Argernon. *Now*. Please. This isn't funny."

"I am not feeling amused any longer."

He moved, stepping up on the bed. Forced by the chain, she had to follow. It was either climb onto the bed willingly or be dragged up by her wrists. Argernon looked up to the ceiling and she followed his gaze. A thick, large hook was affixed to one of the ceiling beams above the bed. Realization set in as she stared at that curved metal. Her glare flew to Argernon.

"No way are you—"

She squealed as he lifted her off her feet by the chain in his fist.

"NO!"

He placed the chain on the hook, leaving Casey to kick air. She was inches from the bed, hanging from the ceiling. The restraints were padded so they didn't dig into her wrists. She wasn't in pain, exactly, but it didn't feel great either to be suspended by her wrists.

Her gaze flew to Argernon as he stepped back to study his work with a nod. His eyes were still narrowed.

"Put me down."

He gave a shake of his head. "Zorn women are taller. Your feet should touch." He turned his head, looking around the room before he looked back at her. "I'll be right back."

Her arms began to hurt from her body hanging. Argernon returned fast with what looked like a small, inches tall drawer. He bent, put it on the floor, and used his arm to shove her legs out of the way as he slid it under her feet. She was able to stand on it.

"Damn it, Argernon. This isn't amusing. Let me down. It hurts."

He sniffed at her then frowned. "Never lie to me. I smell arousal and anger on you, but not pain." He moved closer and reached up, examining the restraints. "You are not in pain. Now you will know punishment for your willful ways."

She tried to kick him, which was hard to do while dangling and trying not to fall off the box she stood on. He easily avoided her foot. Dropping suddenly, he went to his knees in front of her as his hands gripped her calves. Casey gasped as he spread her thighs wide then put them on each of his shoulders, so his face was between her legs. She stared down at him in shock.

"I will not let you come until you plead to me to bury myself inside you."

He curled his arms around her legs, trapping her thighs on his shoulders. His fingers spread her pussy lips wide open, giving him full access to her sex, leaving her exposed and vulnerable to his mouth. With her hanging like she was, she couldn't do anything but buck her hips, trying to avoid his intimate touch. It didn't work. Argernon growled deep in his throat and hot breath hit her, an instant before his tongue was on her clit.

Casey gaped down at him, and he stared right back. Argernon's mouth was open, his wet tongue teasing her clit. The sensation made her clench her teeth to keep from moaning as spasms started in her pussy.

He flicked her over and over again. Pleasure shot through her with every movement. He stopped, tearing his eyes from hers before entering her with his tongue. He had a long, thick tongue that slowly invaded her body, and then withdrew. He growled before doing it again. Then again. Occasionally he'd return to torment her clit.

It was torture. Casey wanted to come badly. Every time she thought she might, he would back off to stare at her swollen, throbbing clit. Then he'd blow hot breath over her, his tongue would enter her briefly or tease her nub again.

This went on seemingly forever. Sweat trickled down her body. Her throat felt dry from her moans and heavy breathing. He wanted her to beg him to fuck her—and she was ready to. She hurt with the need to get off. She knew he could make her climax and Casey needed to come more than she ever remembered needing anything.

His tongue withdrew from her body again. "Do you yield to me, Beautiful? Do you accept me?"

"Asshole!"

He growled—then his lips covered her clit, his mouth totally enclosing her nub.

He sucked on her hard, his tongue lashing against her clit, back and forth with firm pressure. Casey cried out. Her body bowed, on the edge of exploding—

Argernon tore his mouth from her to growl again.

"I can do this for hours. Will you endure it well?"

Tears filled her eyes but she kept them tightly shut. No one could survive this kind of sexual torture. She didn't doubt he could tease and taunt her for hours. Her body literally hurt from need. Her clit throbbed like a painful heartbeat between her legs.

She shook her head and opened her eyes. She had to blink a few times to clear her tears, a few escaping.

"Please, Argernon. I can't take it."

Something flashed in his eyes. He eased his hold on her thighs before gently removing them from his shoulders, until she stood on the drawer with her legs closed.

She fought a sob. He was going to just leave her sexually frustrated, hurting and needy. It was mean and just plain cold.

He climbed to his feet, reached up, and gripped the chain to lift her from the hook.

She moaned softly when he eased her down until her feet touched the bed. His eyes softened as he lowered her arms, and she gasped as the blood flow started to return. His large hands gently massaged her arms and hands. He lowered his body to sit on the bed and he pulled her down beside him.

"I do not like punishing you, Beautiful." Regret flashed in his eyes. He continued rubbing her limbs. "It pains me to do it. I suffered with you. I hurt for you as much as you hurt for me." He glanced at her. "Do you want me to make you come?"

She just stared at him.

The pain in her arms faded away as he rubbed circulation back into her hands—then his hands push her onto her back, the move startling her. Large hands spread her thighs wide open. She looked down at him as he settled on his knees between her legs.

"Stubborn human woman," he growled softly.

Casey threw her head back as Argernon dove for her clit without warning.

His elbows pushed her thighs wider apart as fingers spread her sex for his tongue. Two fingers from his other hand slid deep into her pussy.

Casey cried out as she almost instantly came. The climax tore through her brutally while Argernon sucked on her clit, hammering her with his two digits. She came so hard she was sure it was more than once.

Releasing her clit, he slowly withdrew his fingers. Casey went limp and her eyes closed. She panted in exhaustion. Argernon moved on top of her, his body fitting to hers, careful not to crush her. Opening her eyes, Casey met his intense stare.

"I am in the same condition. I hurt for you," he rasped. Then he entered her.

Casey moaned as Argernon's thick cock pushed inside her. Her pussy was swollen yet slippery wet, so he eased into her easily even though it was a tight fit.

The mere act of entering her and a single thrust was enough. She felt his cock pulsing deep inside as his semen shot into her. He jerked from the power of his release, a groan breaking from his lips, and she watched his face while he came. Sweat trickled down from his forehead as his eyes opened. They stared at each other.

Casey reached up, her chains rattling, cupping his face with both hands. She knew she should slap him but she just wanted to touch him. She didn't understand how he could do what he'd done to either of them, but she *did* believe he'd suffered the sexual frustration right along with her.

The man came instantly upon entering her, just as easily as she'd come for him.

"I hate punishment," he whispered. "We both suffer. Do you understand?"

She did. It made no sense to her but she understood it was a mutual suffering they'd just shared. "Why do it then?"

He blinked. "I am Zorn. You are my bound. You will understand in time."

Casey really doubted it, but she didn't say that out loud.

Argernon shifted. A groan tore from both of them as he started to move slowly, fucking her again. She wound her legs around the backs of his thighs, lifting the chain over his head to allow her to wrap her arms around his neck, and just enjoyed what he was doing to her body. She had to look away from his intense gaze. She couldn't take it when he locked eyes with her while leisurely fucking her. It was too intense emotionally.

His mouth went to her throat, kissing her skin there, licking her.

He made her come again before he slowly withdrew from her body. He didn't remove her restraints. Instead he climbed from the bed as she lay there exhausted. She watched him walk naked to the drawer again. He pulled out another set of chains but she wasn't afraid. She was too tired to get worked up over whatever he might have in mind to do next.

He climbed back onto the bed. Mutely, she watched as he hooked the chain to the top of the headboard then attached it to the one between her wrists. He effectively chained her to the bed.

"I don't trust you, and I'm tired, Casey. It saddens me to do this." He pulled her into his arms as he sighed deeply. "Control, lights off."

The room went dark. Argernon's large, warm body wrapped tighter around hers, spooning her. She was comfortable, the chain long enough that her arms weren't pulled above her head.

She curled her hands at her chest and shut her eyes to fall into an exhausted sleep.

Chapter Six

Casey paced yet again—but only on one side of the bed. The chain wasn't long enough to reach the outer door or the bathroom.

She wondered where Argernon was. Two mornings in a row, he'd awoken her, let her shower and use the bathroom. Then he ate with her before chaining her back up and leaving for hours at a time to work. He'd return with food, release her to use the bathroom, and then he'd leave again.

After two days, she was officially tired of it.

He'd also come up with a new way to torture her—avoidance. He slept fully clothed in the bed they shared and refused to touch her. When she curled into him, she could feel how aroused he was, but he would just roll away, growling at her.

It was also driving her crazy that he was barely speaking to her.

The door opened as Argernon walked in looking tired. He studied her for a second before looking away. In his hand, he held a tray of meats, more weird-looking fruits, and a mug of something dark for her dinner. He headed for the bathroom after putting her food on the edge of the bed. She sat, digging into the food.

Argernon always left the door open to the bathroom, so she watched him strip out of his uniform with his back to her. He had a really nice ass. His back was broad and his arms were muscular. Silky black hair fell to his waist, just teasing the curve of his butt. He stepped into the shower.

This was torture too. She could only watch as he touched his body. Large hands rubbed at his chest as he turned around to face her. He was sporting another major hard-on.

She clenched her teeth, knowing what was going to happen next, since he'd done this every time he came in the door.

He let his hand run lower, his head still thrown back, eyes shut under the water that rained down, making his body slick. He gripped his cock and pumped his shaft as she watched.

Her hand went to the V of her thighs—but stopped at the thick leather pants he'd put on her, belted shut with a thin locked chain. It was the equivalent of a chastity belt; her hand wouldn't even fit between the waist and her belly since he'd pulled them tight. The material was too thick for her to feel her finger rubbing through them.

She was so turned-on as she watched him masturbate. Everything about the damn man turned her on, but watching him come minutes later, hearing him growl as he shot his release in the shower stall, was the worst.

Lowering his head, he turned away from her to let the water wash away the evidence from his body. He waved his hand upward and the water stopped falling. Reaching to turn on the hot air, he slowly turned, lifting his arms to make sure it dried all of him. When his eyes opened, he met her resentful glare. He blinked a few times before walking toward her totally naked, heading for more clothing.

"Feel better?"

He paused, turning his head to glance at her. "Yes."

"Could you at least take these damn pants off me? I'm hot and you have them too tight."

Thick lips twitched with amusement. "You can't pleasure yourself."

Gritting her teeth, she glared at him. "I hate you. You're so damn mean."

"You think I've been mean to you? Have you agreed to be my bound? Have you agreed to come to Zorn with me? No. You have not. The few times I have asked, you have demanded I return you to Earth. We are no longer in orbit, Casey, we have left your planet far behind. My Zorn warriors have found their females and we are on our way home, so you can stop resisting and accept me. We would both be happier."

His gaze roamed down her body, the hungry look burning her. "Wouldn't you like to be naked in bed with me? I would touch you in so many ways while I buried myself in your warm softness over and over. We are both suffering because you are being willful."

"*You* aren't suffering. You're in that shower so much your skin should be pruned."

"I take no real pleasure from self-release. I am Zorn. It is not just a matter of having a vigorous sex drive. My balls would swell and I would get sick if I did not release often. Self-release is a health necessity. My *pleasure* is your body, Beautiful. If you stop being willful and accept all that I offer, we will both be happy."

Defeat made her shoulders droop. "We're really not in orbit over Earth anymore?"

"I told you that already. I did not lie. We are traveling to Zorn. All of my warriors returned from the planet after they had found women to bound with them. "

"So fast? I thought it would take weeks at least."

He was aroused again when he stalked closer to her. She could see ever bare inch of him—including the inches of hardened flesh pointing at her from below his waist. He looked down at her.

"You don't want to know what happens if you do not accept me by the time we reach Zorn."

"Oh, give it to me straight. I'm sure it's something horrible. What happens to me?"

He frowned. "You will be offered to other men, to find one you accept—and if you do not do so quickly, you will be taken by one. Though he may not offer to bound you. He could make you a house helper."

"Like a housekeeper? I'd clean his home?"

He nodded. "And warm his bed. You and his other house helpers would sleep in his bed if he is not bound. If he *is* bound, you would sleep on the bed only if his bound allowed it, or when he is mounting you. If his bound does not allow it, you would be lucky to even have your own room. If you ended up in a poorer household, you would sleep on the floor in the bedroom with the man and his bound. He could and *would* offer your body to guests who came to stay in his home, or he could tire of you and trade you for new home help. In the poorest homes, all the younger males share one woman. The parents can't afford more than one helper for their sons."

She gasped up at him. "That's...horrible! That's how you treat your women? Of all the—"

Argernon growled at her to cut her off. "We're a male-dominant race. Women are weaker physically and smaller than our males. They cannot protect themselves in battle. You have been told how sexual a Zorn warrior is, but you don't know our history. At one time, we nearly destroyed our entire race because our males are ruled by their sex drives. Women were..."

He looked away, clearly uncomfortable, before continuing, "They were harmed, and many were killed. Their numbers dropped radically, until we were in danger of becoming extinct. That is when we devised a system to protect the women. A house helper is protected by the male of the house she lives in. He feeds her, clothes her, and keeps her from harm at the hands of our wilder males, because an unprotected female wouldn't survive without such protection. Much of Zorn is civilized, but some is not, Casey. Any male found abusing a woman is stripped of the right to ever have one under his roof. A man must prove his worthiness to have females, and he must have a safe home for them to live in."

Frowning, Casey stared up at him. "Those women are living, thinking beings. Don't they have *any* say in their lives?"

He hesitated. "Most are raised by their families, and their families will let them choose which male they wished to be protected by. As long as he is worthy to care for her. Many of them end up as helpers in nice homes. Some males will even ask for their helpers' permission or preferences if they wish to take in another. So yes, many women pick the men they are given to, and most house helpers stay in the same houses all of their lives, with the same male."

"What about the ones who don't fall under 'most'?"

His eyes narrowed. "If they are willful, or they cannot produce offspring after being bound, they are less desirable, so they have fewer options. Most men won't tolerate them for long, and will send them away to be someone else's problem."

"I thought this bounding was solid, uh...permanent."

"There are only a few ways to unbound once bound. If a woman is barren, if she has sex with another man after being bound; if her male abuses her, or she tries to kill her bound. Men will sometimes share house helpers with other men, but *never* their bound women."

"What is your definition of abuse?"

"We do not beat our women and we protect them from harm. To not feed or not keep a decent home for a woman is abuse."

Casey frowned at him.

Argernon sighed. "Accept me, Casey, and I will always protect you. I took you from your world, so even if you are barren, even though you wanted me dead and probably still do, I will swear on my honor to remain bound to you." His eyes narrowed. "Even if you let another male touch you, I will keep you." He growled. "But I *will* kill him, and will make you watch him die. If you think I have been mean to you in the past few days, then you will learn a new level of mean if you let another male touch you. Am I clear?"

106

"I thought you said you weren't allowed to beat a woman?"

"I would never beat you. I wouldn't have to."

She swallowed hard at the cold look in his eyes. "I don't know what bound is. I know nothing about your world and I don't even know *you* that well. How can I accept something I don't know a damn thing about? This is unfair!"

"I know this is not fair." The look in his eyes softened, along with his tone. "We have four and a half days to prepare you for your new life. I will tell you everything. Accept me, Casey."

She stared into his eyes. "Give me a couple days to decide. Can we just see how things work out between us? Can't you stop punishing me and just let me get to know you? You're asking me to bind my life to yours until I die. I'd like to spend time with you first before I agree to it."

He didn't look happy but he nodded. "Do not try to kill me, Casey. It would never get you back to Earth, and you would be considered hopelessly willful. You do not ever want to have that label on Zorn. The truly hopeless females end up in med houses."

"Med houses?"

"You do not want to know."

"I asked."

He sighed loudly. "I told you if Zorn males don't release their seed often from their bodies, they get sick. When they do, they are taken to med houses...where women are kept just for that purpose. The females who prove dangerous or who betray their bounds end up there. They are closely regulated by guards, so they cannot be abused, but they are forced to accept any males in need of release, to help cure them."

Shock tore through Casey. "You mean…"

He nodded. "Because you are human, they wouldn't consider it abuse to let more than a few males use your body each day. It is well known on Zorn that human females are very different, so unlike the one or two our females can manage, you might be sent half a dozen males per day. You would not be allowed to refuse—even if they had to bind you to accept those males."

"What kind of screwed-up world do you come from?!"

"Is your Earth perfect? I did research on your planet, Casey. There are so many signals coming from the surface, it was easy to listen to what you call the 'news'. My world isn't at war with itself; we do not have mass deaths fighting each other. We do not spread incurable disease. We do not use women and children as weapons of death. Domestic abuse is very rare and dealt with harshly on Zorn. Not so on Earth."

She nodded sadly. Clearly no world was perfect. "Will you give me a couple days to decide?"

He nodded. "Stand. I'll free you."

She was on her feet immediately. He retrieved the keys to the locks on her restraints and released her wrists, then the chain around the pants. He went to his knees before her and tugged the pants down her legs. The look in his eyes made her wet and hot in seconds. Despite her unwillingness to just instantly commit for life, she still burned for Argernon's touch.

"Lie back on the bed and spread wide for me, Beautiful."

She almost tore her shirt, ripping it from her body as she stepped out of the pants. She was climbing on the bed before she let herself debate the wisdom of succumbing yet again.

She knew she should tell him to go to hell, that she should feel a little ashamed as she stretched out on her back and spread her legs open to display her pussy for him. She promised herself she'd get even with him somehow, later, but for right now, she was hornier than hell, aching—and he owed her *big time* for the last two sexually frustrating days he'd given her.

Argernon's gaze captured hers as he climbed on the bed. "Do you want me inside you or do you want my mouth? What do you need most?"

"Both," she whispered.

He growled, his hands gripping her thighs tightly as his head lowered.

Casey moaned, clawing the bed when his mouth found her clit. He didn't tease her. His lips surrounded the throbbing and swollen flesh, sucking her gently into his mouth as his tongue slid back and forth on her sensitive nub with enough pressure to make her go wild.

"Yes! Oh, Argernon!"

Another growl rumbled from his mouth, vibrating against her clit as his tongue moved faster. He sucked, moving his mouth in a way that tugged on her repeatedly. Two fingers thrust into her pussy and he hooked them, finding the right spot to rub on her G-spot. That was all it took. A scream tore from her lips as the climax hit her, pleasure almost tearing her apart.

He didn't give her time to recover, just releasing her with his mouth and fingers and grabbing her thigh as he slid up her body. He pushed it high, so her knee was trapped by his chest when he lowered on top of her. He didn't need to guide his cock into her. He was rock hard and found her entrance unerringly.

Casey clawed at his shoulders, bucking her hips when Argernon pushed all the way into her, until his balls were against her anus. He started to move in deep, hard thrusts. He adjusted his hips so the angle of his cock rubbed her G-spot with every drive in and out of her.

Frustration made Casey almost scream when Argernon abruptly withdrew and lifted off her.

"Roll over. I want to mount you and fuck you harder."

Eagerly she rolled over, pushing her ass up, her elbows bending to brace against the bed. Without warning, Argernon drove into her from behind. His hands clamped down on her hips, wrapping around them, holding her immobile while he rammed her over and over.

Moans tore from Casey's lips with every slam of his groin against her ass as he drove deep. Pleasure and pain became blurred. One of his hands released her hip to shove between her thighs, thick fingers bracing against her clit, his palm against her lower stomach and the curve of her mound.

His hips increased the pace.

Casey lost it with the added pressure against her clit. Her pussy went wild, clamping down on Argernon, her vaginal walls clenching him like a fist as the orgasm swamped her. Screaming out her pleasure, she came.

Argernon roared, bucking hard against her ass, his seed jetting into her. Collapsing to the bed, they lay entwined together, exhausted.

A few minutes later, Casey opened her eyes. Argernon was staring at her, watching her silently. She couldn't read the emotion on his features but he didn't look angry.

She knew what *she* was thinking. The guy got her off every damn time. It amazed her. He was remarkable with that mouth. His cock was built perfectly to hit every right spot inside her body to make her come. It didn't hurt that he was as sexy as hell. Total eye candy to the max. And those eyes of his were the most beautiful things she'd ever seen. She could stare into them forever. Even his voice turned her on, with its gruffness and how he growled at her often.

"What are you thinking?"

His tongue swiped his lips. "That you're beautiful and you are mine. I won't give you up, Casey. I cannot. You are a part of me, and I don't ever want to leave your body because I want to remain a part of *you*."

She swallowed hard. As far as what a guy was thinking after sex, those were some pretty intense thoughts. No man had ever made her feel as sexy, wanted, or even as needed as Argernon did.

His mouth twisted into a smile. "What are *you* thinking?"

"I'm just thinking about how you make me feel."

A chuckle escaped him. Blue eyes twinkled with amusement. "From your screams of pleasure, you are very fond of me."

She laughed as she swatted his chest. "You think that's funny, do you?"

"Yes." He rolled onto his back.

Grinning, she sat up, putting her hands on his chest to rake her nails lightly over his nipples. She hesitated before she lightly pinched them between her thumbs and fingers.

His body jerked, his blue eyes flaring with passion. She played with the hardening buds as she straddled him, rotating her hips and rubbing against the hard length of him that was thickening more by the second. She was already wet enough, and he grew turned-on enough that she was able to push back when in the right position so he entered her pussy.

Argernon's eyes closed, his grin gone as he moaned softly.

"Not laughing now, are you, Baby?" She rolled her hips in a circle, moving him inside her.

Beautiful eyes snapped open. "Do you want to play?"

"Yes."

"Do you want me to get loud?"

She smiled. "You always get loud. You roar when you come, for Christ's sake."

His hands gripped her hips and he lifted her body off him. He grinned. "I'll be right back."

She sat up, frowning as she watched him almost run into the bathroom. He turned on the shower, letting water pour down his body. He cupped himself, cleaning his groin area particularly well, before he waved off the water. He didn't even waste the seconds it took to dry as he strode quickly into the bedroom to almost jump on the bed. He rolled onto his back, still grinning.

"Play with me. Touch me." He stared at her. "Will you lick me, Casey?"

Her eyes ran over his naked, wet body. He was rock hard again. It was amazing and kind of frightening that the guy rarely got soft. This was a man you didn't laugh at if he said he wanted to fuck a woman to death—because he just might mean it.

Casey straddled his hips again, rested on his lower stomach and letting her attention drift over every inch of his chest. Licking her lips, she bent forward, starting at his neck...

She ran her tongue lightly around his ear, biting the lobe before licking and kissing down to his shoulder, nipping him once more with her teeth, enjoying the taste of his skin.

Argernon growled as his hands gripped her hips.

She leaned back to look at him. "Hands up—and don't touch me."

Glowing blue eyes narrowed. He didn't look happy but he followed directions. He released her with his big, warm hands to put both of his arms up, folding them under the back of his head like a pillow. It really displayed his thick muscles.

Smiling, Casey went for his chest next. She fastened on one nipple, sucking it, while she used her fingernails to lightly play with the other until both of them hardened into pointed tips. A groan sounded from the man under her; his body tensed while his hips arched up a few inches from the bed, lifting both of them.

"Down, Baby," she chuckled, releasing his nipple. "Stay still."

"Patience isn't something I have much of. You turn me on too much. Maybe in a few years, you can play with my body more without me feeling like I will die if I am not inside you."

Years.

Heat swamped her at the thought of having this kind of a sex life for years with Argernon. Was he for real?

She scooted down his body, having to lift up high over his rock-hard erection to sit on his upper thighs. She let her mouth trail kisses over his ribs. She licked him in a few places as well, like the grooves between the muscles on his abs. She let her teeth nip his hipbone.

By the time she reached his thick and throbbing cock, he was growling continuously and his body was tense enough to resemble a sexy statue. His legs shifted slightly apart but didn't move enough to dislodge her.

"Please," he whispered, his voice deep and harsh.

She'd teased him long enough. One of her hands gripped the base of his cock while the other brushed his thigh. She moved to her knees at his side.

"Spread your thighs open so I can get between them."

He instantly moved to obey her. A smile ghosted her lips. She could get used to giving him orders. She looked up at his handsome face, noticing his closed eyes, the passion-pain look, the tight press of his mouth and his sharp fangs hooked on his lower lip, noticeably indenting them. She moved between his thighs slowly, settling down to sit on her legs as she bent forward. Her hand cupped his heavy balls gently, exploring them, caressing the underside with her fingertips.

"Baby?"

Argernon opened his eyes to look down at her. "Yes?" he almost panted.

"Hold still. Don't choke me, okay? You're way big. I like breathing."

Confusion lit his features. "I'd never choke you."

"Not on purpose. Don't move your hips or you will."

Casey lowered her gaze to his cock. She knew there was no way she was going to get him all the way in. She was just glad he'd agreed to hold still. If he thrust up into her mouth while it was wrapped around him, breathing could be a slight issue. She wet her lips again, moistening her mouth.

She licked the large, round tip of him first, and swirled her tongue around his mushroomed head.

The taste of him was a massive surprise.

More pre-cum beaded on the tiny slit on his cock, and to make sure she was really tasting what she thought she had, Casey ran her tongue over him again, tracing that little crevice. A growl tore from Argernon.

He tasted really sweet—like warm, melted sugar of some sort.

He was *delicious*.

More pre-cum eased from his cock and Casey eagerly caught it on her tongue. She moaned, taking more of him into her mouth. It was a taste she could get addicted to. She had a feeling if he tasted that good at the end, he'd become her favorite dessert anytime she had a sweet craving.

The circumference of his cock barely fit in her mouth. Once she was past the thicker head, his shaft thinned slightly, but not by much, before it grew thick again. She greedily sucked as much of him as she could.

She heard Argernon gasp. His body moved slightly but he didn't thrust into her mouth. He squirmed under her while growling in a low tone that sounded more animal than man. She heard him panting louder and louder until he sounded like he was having difficulty breathing as she continued to suck and lick him. She took him as deep as she could, swallowing rapidly before lifting up, turning her head, and then taking him deep again at the new angle.

"Casey!" he snarled.

It was the only warning she got before his cock swelled slightly and he was coming hard down her throat. Sweetness filled her mouth. She moaned in surprise and delight at the taste of him, swallowing everything he had to give.

Casey had thought his pre-cum was sweet, but he tasted even better when he came. She milked him with her mouth, moaning the entire time, then cleaned every inch until she reached the head of his shaft, taking every drop hidden there.

Easing him out of her mouth at last, she ran the tip of her tongue over her lips. She knew what he reminded her of now. He tasted like a mix of honey and brown sugar, melted together. It amazed her.

Rising on her knees, she peered at Argernon.

His head was thrown back so far, all she could see was his neck. She could hear him breathing hard still, panting. One hand gripped the bedding by his hip, and she was stunned to see he'd torn the material with his fisted hand. His other hand was on his chest.

The sight of his blood made her gasp.

She climbed up him to grab his bleeding hand, cradling it, wondering what had happened. Her eyes flew to his face. That's when she saw the blood on his lower lip and chin. Really alarmed now, she examined his hand—and saw the small holes that caused the bleeding. They were bite marks from his teeth.

"Why did you bite yourself?"

His sexy eyes opened. Amazement and satisfaction literally glowed from their depths as his full mouth curved into a grin. "You told me not to move. I wanted to so badly, I bit myself to keep still. I knew with your teeth around me, startling you with my roar of pleasure wouldn't be a smart thing to do. Lord of the Moons. That was..." He chuckled. "It's a good thing you're my bound. You definitely would be now, if you were not before." His uninjured hand moved to rub her stomach in a soft caress. Wonder-filled eyes rose to hers. "You took my seed down your throat. I am in awe of you, Beautiful. You honor me more than any woman ever has."

She blinked then let his words sink in. "Okay."

A grin split his lips widely, a look of ecstasy taking over his face. "Zorn women don't swallow seed. You must really be fond of me to accept my seed in that way. You accept me as your bound. I will make you happy, Beautiful."

Casey had to slam her mouth shut. It had fallen open. "Your women don't swallow?"

He couldn't wipe the grin from his face. He shook his head. "They lick the *hais* but move away when seed spills. But *you*...you took me into your mouth and you took my seed into your belly." His hand caressed her stomach again. "Lord of the Moons, did that feel so good."

"Wow. For a world with highly sexual men, you guys don't do a lot."

"What do you mean?"

"You don't have anal sex, and now you're telling me your women don't give blow jobs? They give lick-and-flee?"

He chuckled. "It is not called lick and flee. It is called tonguing. I assume what you just did to me is called a blow job? You didn't blow on me, so why is it called that?"

She laughed. "Hell if I know. Maybe it's because it blows a guy's mind?"

He laughed harder as he pulled her down on his body. "My mind is blown. I know this saying. Now I think I know what you must feel when I am tonguing your clit. I will do that to you a lot more. I was worried the

118

first time I touched you that I would do it wrong. I am a fast learner though, and you enjoy it as much as I hoped you would."

"Back up." Casey stared down at him in confusion. "What do you mean, you were worried you'd do it wrong and you had to learn fast?"

He gazed at her fondly. "You are slightly different from Zorn females. Their *unis* is deep inside and can't be tongued. Your *unis*, clit, is very accessible. My brother told me about human women, and what to do with one, since he learned from his bound. What he did *not* tell me is how good you would taste, and how much it would excite me to tongue you and hear you respond to me. Do I do it well? You seem to enjoy my mouth on you."

She was stunned. "You learn *really* fast."

He tilted his head slightly, staring at her. "What is that look in your eyes? Tell me what you are thinking."

She slowly smiled. "I was just thinking that it's kind of funny that a guy who's never touched a human woman—and who had never tongued one—is the best lover I've ever had." She stroked his chest. "Some Earth guys should take lessons from you Zorn men. A lot of them couldn't find a clit even with a map drawn for them—and have no clue what to do with one when they find it."

He chuckled. "Maybe we should send Zorn women to your men."

Chapter Seven

Casey surreptitiously stared at Argernon during dinner the next day. They were sitting on the bed, facing each other with their trays between them. He'd just come in from his work shift. She was nervous...but she'd had all day to think while he'd been gone.

Argernon arched an eyebrow. "What are you thinking about? You look very stern."

"I have questions."

"I was told that humans are very curious. Proceed with your questions."

She smiled. He looked ready to do battle, judging by his grim expression and tense shoulders. "Relax. This isn't going to be painful."

"I don't know about that. My brother warned me that his bound gets angry with him for reasons he sometimes can't understand when he answers her questions."

"That sounds ominous. Uh-oh. Do you know what they fight about? Maybe we can start there. I want to know the good and the bad about this bound thing."

He hesitated. "She refuses to be naked for him outside their bedroom."

Eyebrows shot up. "Naked?"

"She is not comfortable naked in his home, but that is the Zorn way. Our women only cover their bodies when they leave the house or when guests are over. Weather permitting, as well."

"And you want me naked when we're at home together?"

He laughed. "What do *you* think?"

She grinned. "I might run around naked." She winked. "It would save time getting undressed."

He grinned widely at her. "I knew you were perfect for me."

"Okay. We're getting somewhere. What else do they fight about?"

His grin died a fast death. "She doesn't like it that she can't go outside without guards and without his protection. You will have to stay in our home, where it is safe. Human women are much wanted on Zorn. I told you how our males are. Four attackers went after my brother's bound in their home, and would have killed her after forcing her to take them inside her body. You will not be permitted to go anywhere alone, but I have a beautiful home with a large yard and nice view, where you will be safe. I will take you places often so you will not be lonely or bored."

Casey digested that. "Okay. I can see the danger and appreciate that it wouldn't be safe for me as a human to walk around by myself. I can live with that, as long as I don't have to sit staring at walls all the time. I don't want to go house crazy."

"No argument?"

"Not so far. What other fights do they have?"

He hesitated. "She was very upset when my father sent a woman to my brother."

That brought a frown to her face. "Why did your father send a woman to your brother?"

"My father was not happy that my brother bound to a human at first, so he sent my brother a very desirable Zorn woman, who many men wanted. He thought she would tempt my brother from his bound human woman, but he was not tempted at all."

"Is your father going to pull that shit with us?"

He shook his head. "No. He learned his lesson. He will not be sending women to our home to try to bound me to a Zorn female instead." He hesitated. "But there is something I need to explain to you."

"Okay." She studied him warily.

Argernon hesitated. "I did not intend to search for a human, much less bound one. Before I left, I did not make any arrangements to bring you home. I—"

A loud blasting sound pierced the room.

Casey gasped, throwing her hands up over her ears to mute some of the painfully loud noises. Argernon leapt from the bed, running for the door.

"Stay!" he roared at her.

He was gone that fast.

The blasting sounds blared through the room loudly, over and over again, hurting Casey's ears even when muffled by her hands. Whatever that alarm was, she hadn't liked the look on Argernon's face as he'd jumped from the bed to run from the room. He'd been shirtless, and a quick check of the floor, where she saw his boots, confirmed he was barefoot too.

She grab for a pillow, shoving her head under it to dull the loud blasts, her worry for Argernon mounting.

The sound suddenly went silent.

Casey sat up, biting her lip, wondering what in the hell was going on. Obviously it had to be something bad and urgent. She sat in the middle of the bed, hugging the pillow to her chest; the not knowing and wondering were awful. She hated being left clueless.

Then terror hit Casey as she heard a noise that sounded like a muffled explosion just before the entire room shook, as if an earthquake had hit.

She sat for seconds in shock before climbing off the bed, backing against the wall when she felt the floor vibrating strongly beneath her. It certainly hadn't done *that* before. But she didn't even have time to wonder what was causing it—all she could do was cry out as a loud alarm blared again just as her feet left the floor entirely.

Horror hit her as she realized what was going on. The gravity on the ship was gone.

Her hands clawed at the wall for purchase but she couldn't find anything to grasp on the slick surface. The sensation of weightlessness was incredibly disconcerting, and she panicked further when she noticed things from the room floating around her.

She pushed at the wall but then screamed when she immediately realized her mistake and started to spin. She went upside down and the world went even crazier as she flipped. Groaning, she rolled again, grabbing for the bedsheets, her hand fisting the material. It slowed then stopped her momentum but relief was short-lived. The sheet started to pull from the mattress slowly, making Casey drift higher and higher, until she was almost to the ceiling.

She grabbed another fistful and yanked frantically with both hands, managing to lower herself slightly. She was sobbing now, terrified. Where was the gravity? Had that sound really been an explosion? Had the ship crashed? Had the engine blown up? Jesus, they were in *space*! What would happen to them without an engine?

All those thoughts flew through her head in rapid succession.

She grabbed for the headboard when she drifted close enough. As her fingers gripped it, she sighed in relief. The bed had to be somehow bolted down because it was still attached firmly to the floor. The mattresses stayed put, so they had to be anchored as well. She clutched the headboard with both hands and maneuvered her body—painstakingly slowly—until she'd managed to get her ass on the mattress with her body curled against the headboard.

She didn't dare release her hold on the headboard to wipe at her tears. Perhaps the weirdest part was that she saw a few of her tears drifting in front of her. They hadn't slipped down her cheeks. They'd simply floated away.

"Oh God," she muttered, not knowing if she was cursing what was happening or starting a prayer. All she knew was that she was scared and Argernon was out there somewhere. Was he alive? Had that explosion been near him? She didn't know.

Her next thoughts were even worse. What if she was the only survivor? Would the oxygen run out? Would she starve to death? Would she die drifting in space on a damaged ship?

She just wanted Argernon to come for her, to tell her what was going on. She wanted him to tell her that everything was all right. She wanted *him* to be all right.

Casey continued to hug the headboard as time passed. It seemed like hours went by at a snail's pace.

The lights flickered and she moaned. "Not a good sign."

They flicked on and off a few more times, then finally they went out and stayed out, leaving her in terrifying utter darkness.

She clung to the bed, listening to the silence, her arms starting to ache from anchoring her body. Something bumped her, making her scream. She frantically grabbed at whatever it was that had brushed her back.

A hysterical laugh escaped when she realized it was one of Argernon's boots.

She pushed it away, thinking about all the floating things in the room. She knew more stuff would probably touch her occasionally, and she tried to prepare for the inevitable so she didn't scream again.

The ship felt oddly dead, now that the vibrations were gone and there was no sound whatsoever. She jerked awake when she started to float away from the headboard, the slight tug on her hand waking her, so she gripped tighter, trying to stay alert. Taking deep breaths, she realized there still seemed to be plenty of air, which was a good sign. She hoped, anyway.

Her thoughts centered once more on Argernon, wondering if he was alive still, and if so, why he hadn't come for her. The thought of something happening to him had grief slamming into her chest.

A slight noise drew her attention. She listened, heard it again, and strained to hear the faint *thunk*, and then another. She realized the noise was getting closer, until she could have sworn it was right outside the door.

Her eyes went in that direction, unable to really see anything in the darkness.

A loud sound made her jump. Metal hitting metal. Then a *pop* similar to a balloon bursting.

Light blinded her next—a bright, long, thin crack of it. The door opened wider and more brightness spilled in.

"Thank God," she almost moaned as she saw someone pushing the door open.

It wasn't Argernon but a stranger. He held some kind of light that illuminated everything in a wide circle around him.

The male had long red hair, but it wasn't the one she'd met before, and he was shirtless, with blood smeared on his stomach. Fear crawled

126

over Casey. His eyes were so dark they looked black, but it could have been because she couldn't see his face that well. He growled at her as he moved into the room.

Thunk. Thunk. Thunk.

Her eyes flew to his feet. He wore metal-covered boots that made that loud sound as he walked across the floor. Some kind of gravity boots, she had to assume, since he wasn't floating. He reached the side of the bed and held out his hand. She saw blood but she reached for it anyway. Up close, she could see some cuts on his stomach. His knuckles were also scraped, as if he'd hit something. His large hand wrapped around hers and as he pulled her away from the bed, she let go of the headboard.

"What happened? Where's Argernon?" She tried to ignore the sick feeling of being weightless and floating as he slowly maneuvered her onto his back.

He growled. The power was out so she guessed the translator didn't work. Frustration hit. It was like being back in the cave with Argernon, when they couldn't communicate.

The large man wrapped her arm under his and curled her hand over his shoulder. He nodded his head toward his other arm and she grasped his other side. He turned with Casey floating behind him, gripping him hard as he started the jerky walk out of the room into the corridor.

"Where are you taking me?" Her voice shook. "Is Argernon all right?"

The man didn't pause. He ignored her as he slowly walked down the corridor, so she stayed quiet and let him concentrate on getting them down the hall. It was obvious he struggled with the uncomfortable and heavy boots. He finally made it to a ladder that led up to a hatch, a circular shape about four feet in circumference. Casey looked up, seeing light and another male peering down at them from the open hatch.

The redhead turned to look at Casey, softly growling at her while pointing. His hand gripped hers on one of his shoulders to gently pry her fingers loose. She understood, letting him go. He gave her a push toward the hatch a good ten feet above their heads.

A squeal escaped as she floating in the air, without anything anchoring her. Kicking her arms and legs didn't do a damn thing; she was at gravity's mercy as she slowly ascended to the hatch. Below her, she could've sworn she heard the redhead laugh. It was almost comforting that he found it amusing she was freaking out. If they were dying, he wouldn't be laughing at her, right? She could only hope.

The man above leaned down to grab her hands as soon as she was within reach. She stared up into the face of a black-haired male with glowing green eyes who wasn't Argernon either. Another stranger.

Uncertainty hit her. Were they with Argernon? Or had the ship been boarded by other Zorn? Maybe they were a rescue team. She couldn't be sure, but she thought they might be moving from one ship to another through the hatch.

The man pulled her the rest of the way through the opening by one arm, fisting her clothes at the waist when she was clear of the hatch. He wore boots like the redhead below. She met his eyes.

"Argernon? Is he all right?"

The man blinked in confusion, clearly showing that he didn't understand.

She gripped her shirt, loudly sniffed it and stared at the man. "Argernon?"

She knew the material smelled like Argernon, since it was his discarded one from the day before, and she knew they had a good sense of smell. The man seemed to understand. She saw something in his eyes that made tears well in her own.

Pity.

"Oh God. He's dead, isn't he?" She grabbed the man by the front of his shirt. "Is he dead?" Her voice rose, knowing she was about to start sobbing.

The man cupped her face, leaning in, and he looked like he was going to kiss her.

Alarmed, Casey jerked her head back.

He expression turned amused and he chuckled as he secured her arms around his neck and began walking again, keeping his hands respectfully at her waist as they went down a corridor. She looked over his shoulder toward the hatch but the redhead hadn't followed them up.

The man continued down a couple more corridors before pausing at a door, which he forced open by cranking a handle. She adjusted her hold to avoid impeding his progress, then stared wide-eyed at the large room he walked into that looked like a massive cargo area, most of it shadowed in darkness. No, they definitely weren't on the smaller vessel any longer. This had to be the Zorn ship they'd docked with, the one Argernon had mentioned. Casey saw lights inside the high windows of a small ship but couldn't see anything moving inside.

He headed for the ship, lurching up a wide ramp in his awkward boots. Once they were inside, she took in a well-lit, small room with another door. The man reached to push a large button on the wall and the ramp started to lift, closing with a loud *clang*.

The man suddenly gripped her, pulled her tight to his body and wrapped his arms around her, meeting her frightened gaze. Casey heard a beeping sound...

And if the man hadn't been holding her in his arms, she would have slammed hard into the floor as gravity returned instantly.

The man tensed hard, bracing himself and taking her weight, before easing her onto her feet.

She stumbled when he released her. Her body felt unbearably heavy after being weightless for so long. She dizzily watched the man bend over to do something to the boots before stepping out of them. Barefoot, he straightened up to his full height of about six-three and pointed to the doors behind her. She turned around as he stepped close and hit another button, and those doors slid open.

The interior of the ship wasn't that large. She was stunned to see they weren't alone. A thin brunette human woman was sitting on a bench seat, looking scared. Something close to relief hit Casey as their gazes met.

The woman stood up instantly. "You're human!"

"Yes," Casey said before glaring up at the man who'd brought her to the shuttle. "What's going on? Where's Argernon?"

"Calm down. I'm Rachael Dean," she said softly. "Don't yell. They don't understand us. I don't think the computers in here have the program the Zorn run to communicate with us, and they obviously don't have the implants in their ears."

Casey's gaze shot back to the woman. "Do *you* know what's going on?"

"No. I was locked in my room until one of them showed up." Casey thought she saw a flicker of fear as Rachael said, "I don't think they're Zorn. Look at his face...you'll see differences. For instance, these guys have pointed ears."

Her stomach dropped as Casey studied the tall man who had brought her to the shuttle. Rachael was right. The guy's eyes were slanted slightly, and he did have pointed ears. She also noticed he had spots on the backs of his hands. Argernon didn't have any of that.

She was pretty sure that these men weren't Zorn, too.

"Shit." Casey took a step away from the guy, quickly realizing she had nowhere to flee to except the back of the ship—where two men were standing, blocking the only other door. She hadn't noticed them before. Maybe they'd just entered.

She stared up at the man who'd brought her here. "What do you want? Can you understand me?"

The tall man stepped forward to invade Casey's personal space. A growl rumbled from his throat and he gave her a cold look when she took a step away. She glared back at him, trying to not to let him see her terror.

He moved closer, almost touching Casey now, to snarl something at her. He was showing sharp teeth. His tone wasn't friendly. Behind her Rachael softly cursed.

"Don't look down but that guy is turned-on big time."

Casey's gaze jerked down to the front of his pants. She couldn't help it. Fear hit her hard at the sight of the guy's obvious state of arousal. He was turned-on big time, all right. She backed up more, right into Rachael, who gently gripped her. Turning her head, Casey eyed the other two men in the shuttle; both of the large males were staring intently at Casey and Rachael.

"We are in deep shit," Rachael whispered.

"Just stay calm." It was good advice but even Casey was having a hard time following her own words. Where was Argernon and who were these men? Had they attacked the ship? It seemed really damn likely. "I think they might be space pirates."

"Great. Just fucking great," Rachael almost sobbed. "First I got drunk in a bar, ended up in bed with this big son of a bitch who could fuck like a machine, and then I woke up on a spaceship with said machine telling me I was the equivalent of his wife. Now *this* shit. Do you think they're going to kill us?"

"I don't know. I hope not."

Rachael sniffed. "I just want to go home. The guy who grabbed me is nice and he's hell on wheels in bed but I didn't sign up for this shit. I just wanted to have a good time and he looked like a great lay. Were you picked up at a bar too?"

"No."

Casey tensed as she saw the two men in the back start to move forward. One of them reached for the front of his pants—always a bad sign—his full focus locked on Rachael.

"Listen to me, Rachael. Do you know how to fight?"

The woman gripped Casey tighter and shook. "No. Why?"

Casey swallowed hard. "That one is undressing, and so is his friend now. Which is damn bad."

Rachael's head swung toward the back of the shuttle and she whimpered. "Oh God! Don't fight. Maybe they won't hurt us too much. They always say to not fight your attackers."

Rage hit Casey. She glared at man who'd brought her into the shuttle, despite the dread hitting her when he began to remove his shirt slowly, his eyes locked on her breasts.

The three men were going to rape them.

"I'm not going to let this happen without a fight."

"Are you nuts?" Rachael gasped. "They're like seven feet tall and built like linebackers! It would be like punching a brick wall if you hit one of them."

"They aren't seven feet tall, and they aren't as muscular as Argernon, so maybe they aren't as strong. Are you with me?"

"You're crazy." Rachael released her to back away.

Casey focused on the man in front of her. He opened his pants and pointed at her, snarling and motioning to her clothes. She knew he was demanding she take them off.

She shook her head. No way was she going to strip and make things easier for him. Her mind worked frantically. Attackers rarely expected women to fight back.

The other two men lunged forward, both grabbing Rachael by her arms, lifting her. Casey was stunned for precious seconds as she jerked her head around to see the two large males carrying a kicking and screaming Rachael toward the back of the shuttle by her arms, both men totally naked.

Casey instantly tried to go to Rachael's aid. She even took a step— before a large hand gripped her arm, spinning her around violently.

She yanked out of his hold, stumbling back, glaring at him.

The man growled at Casey, showing sharp yellow teeth. His eyes narrowed as his nostrils flared—

And Casey lunged at him, turning just before she hit his body, making him stumble as her shoulder hit his ribs hard.

He obviously hadn't expected her to do that, catching him off guard. They both went crashing to the shuttle floor, Casey landing on top of the man.

He gasped as she slammed her knee into his groin as hard as she could.

She knew he had nuts. Argernon had them, and this guy was humanoid too. And the fact that he hissed out in pain a second after her knee slammed into the vee of his thighs proved that he definitely had something there to hit.

The alien threw her off him to curl into a protective ball, groaning as he cupped the front of his pants.

She rolled across the floor, slamming into benches, knowing they were going to leave bruises on her body, but she forced herself to stand up.

Rachael's scream rang in her ears. Casey saw the other two men pinning the woman to the floor at the back of the shuttle. With their free hands, they were tearing at her shirt, their attention fixed as they stripped the struggling woman. She was screaming and trying to fight them off but her blows didn't even make them flinch.

With their backs to Casey, they hadn't seen what she'd done to her attacker.

Casey didn't think. She screamed, running at the two men to try to stop them from raping Rachael.

One of them began to turn just as she launched herself at him. She hit the man's back, her fingers clawing. He tensed, managing not to fall over when Casey's body hit his, flattening against him. Her fingernails found purchase in his flesh, clawing frantically as she dug into his skin, making him roar out in pain.

He twisted hard, flinging Casey away.

She rolled across the shuttle floor once again and came to a halt when her body slammed into an unforgiving surface. A wall had stopped her this time, leaving her sprawled on her stomach. Her hip hurt the worst, followed by the pain in her elbow.

She lifted her head to watch the man she'd attacked staggering to his feet. She saw blood on his arm coming from the fresh claw marks at his shoulder, where she'd gotten him good. Rage filled his expression when he stood at his full height.

Behind him, his friend turned his attention on Casey too.

It gave Rachael a fighting chance. She struggled to sit, bare from the waist up.

Then Rachael screamed—looking positively crazy with terror.

The man still gripping her thigh turned just as Rachael clawed at his face with her fingernails.

The man roared and struck out blindly with his fist.

Casey saw it happen almost too quickly for her eyes to follow.

The man punched Rachael. He was strong and his fist slammed brutally into her face, square at her mouth and nose. A horrible crunching noise came from the impact. Blood flew as Rachael's head snapped back, her body flung flat to the floor.

Everything inside the shuttle seemed to freeze, even time.

The man who'd been approaching Casey turned slowly, staring at Rachael's still form. The man who'd hit her scrambled back in obvious horror. Blood ran down his face from the claw marks along both of his cheeks.

Casey was stunned for long seconds before she began to move, crawling to Rachael. Neither of the two men stopped her and Casey crawled faster, her entire body shaking badly by the time she reached the woman. She stared down at her, momentarily speechless.

"Oh God!"

Hot tears fell down Casey's face.

Rachael was dead. Her lifeless eyes were open, staring at the ceiling of the shuttle. Her nose was broken; blood seeped down her face from her mouth and nose, and her jaw looked broken as well.

With shaking hands, Casey touched Rachael's warm skin at her throat to search for a pulse, already knowing it was futile—and felt nothing. Rachael was definitely dead.

Casey turned to stare in horror at the man who had punched Rachael. He looked slightly pale as he met her gaze. He crawled back further, shaking his head.

"You son of a bitch. You killed her! *You really killed her!*"

She heard growling, and whipped her head toward the scary sound.

The man she'd taken down with a knee to the crotch was getting to his feet. He was the one growling. Then he roared suddenly, storming straight for Casey and Rachael.

She knew her life was over. These men were rapists and killers.

But the man ignored Casey entirely as he moved around her. He bent over Rachael's body, staring down at the dead woman's face. He put his hand to her throat, snarling, before he lifted his head.

Pure rage gripped his features—all of it directed at the man who'd killed Rachael.

The enraged man moved fast, lunging over Rachael's body to grab her killer by the throat. The infuriated alien hauled the naked man to his feet, another roar tearing through the shuttle a second before he threw Rachael's killer. His body went flying until he hit the far wall of the shuttle. The man crumpled to the floor after bouncing off the wall. His attacker snarled again.

Casey was in shock. She watched all three men snarl at each other. They were obviously arguing. They ignored her completely, so she swiftly picked up a discarded shirt from one of the men who had attacked Rachael. Her hand shook as she closed the other woman's eyes, covering up her face and breasts with the shirt.

The men started to fight. Casey couldn't believe the scene unfolding before her as the two naked aliens attacked the one who'd brought her to the shuttle. They went to the floor in a dog pile of large bodies and fists.

Casey jumped to her feet, her legs shaky. The back of the shuttle was just feet away.

She moved fast, not thinking, knowing she didn't have time for that luxury. She hadn't heard the shuttle engines come on, so they were still in the Zorn ship.

She ran for the back door, which automatically opened for her.

She was in a duplicate of the room at the front of the shuttle, the one where gravity had been restored. The doors slammed shut behind her and she frantically looked around the small area. She saw a large button and dove for it, hitting it as hard as she could. A loud buzz sounded and seconds later, the outer doors opened, a ramp descending. Casey expected to float out the door into zero gravity, but she didn't. Cautiously, she moved forward, stepping out of the smaller ship.

Gravity had been restored in the Zorn ship and the lights were back on.

Casey ran.

She had no idea where she was going, but she wanted to get away from those men. She bolted for the door they'd come through earlier, feeling relief when it automatically opened for her this time.

She ended up in a corridor and she sprinting until she found an intersection. She'd been rattled when she'd come through earlier but she thought she remembered the corridors they'd traveled down. She was pretty sure she was going in the right direction.

Either way, she had to keep going. Somewhere on the ship was Argernon.

Chapter Eight

Casey's side hurt. She was hopelessly lost and she hadn't run into anyone. She'd found a hatch and had crawled down a floor, hoping it led back to the small jumper, but instead it was another level of the huge ship. Where were the Zorn men?

With the eerie silence fraying her nerves, she was more afraid of running into the men who *weren't* Zorn. If the ones she'd escaped from were tracking her, they hadn't found her yet.

She was pretty sure she was in some kind of crew quarters area. She tried to find a place to hide but there wasn't anywhere to go. None of the doors opened on this level, though she touched every pad she saw, just in case. The only one that opened automatically just led from one corridor to another.

With her feet bare, she couldn't miss the slight vibration of the floor under her, indicating that the ship was moving again. She didn't know if she should be relieved or scared. Maybe the Zorn had control of their ship again...but maybe not.

She heard growling right before movement flashed in the corner of her eye as she was about to round yet another corner.

Quickly stepping back, she peeked around to the next corridor to see a man walking toward her dressed in black clothes, similar to Argernon's. He was looking at some kind of tablet thing in his hands, his attention so focused he didn't see her. His heavy-duty black boots were also just like the ones Argernon wore, and he looked Zorn. Casey's eyes flew to his ears peeking out of long black hair that was half pulled back from his face, noting that they were definitely round.

"Hey, you!" Casey called out. She ran toward him.

He stopped walking as his head snapped up. He froze for just a second, looking almost surprised to see her, but then he recovered quickly, moving toward her. Casey was sure he was Zorn by the time they'd both stopped a few feet in front of each other. She met his glowing green gaze, and joy filled her at the sight.

"Can you understand me? Do you have one of those implant things?"

The man nodded. He reached out his hand, holding it out to her palm up.

Casey hesitated. "Where is Argernon?"

He stretched his hand closer to her. Casey eyed it and then lifted her gaze to his. "Will you take me to Argernon?"

Relief overwhelmed her when he nodded. She put her hand in his larger one and he slowly turned, tugging on her, so she followed him when he led her to a *conis* on the wall. He was probably turning on the translator, which made her ecstatic, because she wanted to be able to talk so badly. A hundred questions filled her head.

But the man just pressed a button and growled into the built-in device. Seconds later, someone growled back. The man released the button and his gaze scanned the corridor in both directions. He looked on-guard to her, tense, as if he was expecting trouble.

She heard faint growling minutes later—but it wasn't from the man gripping her hand.

Casey turned, staring down the corridor, to see Argernon coming at her fast. He was still barefoot and bare-chested, and had two other Zorn men walking right behind him. His gaze met with hers.

Sheer happiness at seeing Argernon alive and well slammed into Casey. She swore the man gripping her hand chuckled as he released his hold.

In the next instant, Argernon had yanked her against him tightly.

She slammed into his bare chest, not even caring that he was sweaty. Her arms went around his waist as she hugged him almost as tightly as his crushing arms held her. His entire body seemed to quiver when he lowered his head to nuzzle her hair with his jaw.

She didn't want to let him go but forced herself to step back to look at him, seeing relief in his expression, and a few other emotions she couldn't guess. Mostly she saw his happiness, and she was damn happy to see him again too.

He studied her face first, and then started to examine her with his hands while continuing his visually inspection her body. After sniffing at her a few times, he snarled at one of his men. They snarled back. Argernon looked enraged.

One of the men tore open the *conis* panel to start working on it with a cumbersome-looking tool. He softly growled something and then there was a beep.

"I don't care," Argernon snarled. "Fix it *right now*! I want to know what happened to her. She should have been safe, locked in my room. I smell Collis on her!"

"I'm trying to fix it, Argis Argernon," a male growled. "We're a mess. Gravity is restored and we're moving again. I got us up to full power but we're still having problems with some of our systems. They fried us when they attacked and our internal sensors are shot. I think we killed them all, but the lockdown procedure should be operational, so if some of the Collis *are* still onboard, hopefully we've trapped them, wherever they are."

"Just fix it soon." Argernon looked really pissed off. "I want to make sure my bound is unharmed. She's scenting fear, she was wandering the ship, and she came in contact with a Collis! Make it a priority. I can't stand not being able to talk to her!"

"Argernon?" Casey stared up at him.

His head lowered. "Yes, Beautiful? I wish you could understand me."

"But...I can."

He blinked in surprise. A second later he smiled. "You can? The *conis* is working?"

"Yes. What in the hell is going on? And if Collis are men with pointed ears, spots on the backs of their hands, and they look kind of like Zorn, then I definitely met them. They took me from your room and took me to some little shuttle. I escaped."

Argernon's mouth dropped open. He paled. "What?"

She fought tears. "They had another human woman there. They killed her, Argernon! They were going to rape us. I fought. She tried to fight. One of them punched her in the face when she clawed him. He hit her too hard and killed her. Then the three men started to fight each other and I got away. I've been searching the ship looking for you but none of the doors open and I didn't see anyone until that guy found me."

Argernon snarled. The translator remained quiet. He jerked his head around to glare at one of his men. "We need to search every inch of the ship and find these betrayers *now*!"

He turned his full attention on her. He caressed her cheek. "Did they hurt you? Tell me the truth."

"I got away before they could really do anything to me."

Relief washed over his face. "We were attacked by the Collis. We're not at war with them, so we don't know why they did it. They live on a planet not far from Zorn. We thought they'd used just one shuttle, but we have that one secured. If they took *you* to a shuttle, that means there's another one. Several internal sensors are down so we can't track anyone inside until it's fixed. But we initiated lockdown, so without a palm print, it should seal off the ship at every junction."

"It's not working. At least not for all the doors. I couldn't get into any rooms but I was able to walk around. The doors to all the closed corridors automatically opened for me."

Argernon snarled again, turning his head to glare at his men. "Fix it now and alert everyone that lockdown is nonfunctional. Order our men to search the ship for those betraying Collis."

144

"Yes, Argis Argernon. I'm sending out the alerts now." The man at the panel was typing something into it.

Argernon's gaze returned to Casey. "I thought you were safe in my room. I am sorry. If I had known you were in danger, I would have been there." His shoulders slumped. "I failed to protect you."

"It wasn't your fault. Really."

He dropped to his knees in front of her. Casey held still as Argernon started sniffing at her, pressing his nose against her shirt—then growls tore from him, the sounds vicious. His hands fisted her shirt as his head snapped up.

"I smell more than one male on you."

She swallowed. "One of them took me from the room. I attacked another and landed on top of him. I'm fine, Argernon."

He climbed to his feet, a look of fury hardening his features. "You're my bound. I should have protected you better. I will never be remiss again, Casey. I swear it to you! Do you forgive me?"

She nodded. He was beating himself up over something that wasn't his fault.

She heard a loud beeping sound.

Argernon spun around to face his men. "What is it?"

"We have a breach on deck three," one of his men snarled. "It looks like they aren't done yet. They are heading right for us. I've sent an alert and our males are on their way."

Argernon shoved Casey none too gently against a wall and moved in front of her, trapping her body with his larger one. Her new best friend, fear, swamped her as she stared at Argernon's wide back.

She heard the Collis before she saw them. They were wearing those metal boots that clanked loudly on the corridor floor. Casey did a head count on the Collis as the pointy-eared aliens paused—seven. The one in front was the one she'd attacked in the shuttle, and she saw the two men who had attacked Rachael behind him.

"That's him, leading them," Casey whispered. "He's the one I attacked because he was going to rape me. The two shirtless men behind him are the ones who killed Rachael."

"Stay put and don't move." Argernon's voice was hard to understand since he snarled the words so harshly. "The leader is mine." Argernon threw his head back, a roar tearing from his throat. "You will die for attacking my ship!"

The other man roared back. "We want the Earth women. They are worth a fortune. Give us the females—all of them—and we'll leave you lowly Zorn alive."

"How did they know we carried humans aboard?" It was the man who had fixed the *conis*. His voice was soft, so it didn't carry.

"I don't know," Argernon spat. "But it's the last thing they will do after they tried to steal my bound. Kill them all!"

Casey gasped as Argernon roared again—then suddenly he was gone from in front of her, leaping forward, literally, to attack the alien who had tried to rape her.

The man's face paled before Argernon was on him. Both of them went flying backward into the other Collis men. Argernon's three warriors were in the fight an instant later. Four Zorn against seven Collis.

Helplessness hit Casey while she watched the men fighting, Argernon quickly getting lost in a pile of moving bodies and vicious snarls. But it seemed clear the Zorn men were much stronger than the Collis. Casey figured that out fast as she watched one of Argernon's men grab hold of a Collis, slamming his enemy hard against the wall, the crack of breaking bones reaching her ears. The Collis screamed in pain before going airborne when the Zorn man tossed him.

The Collis went sailing past Casey down the corridor, where he landed hard about six feet from her.

Her attention turned back to the fight. Argernon was on top of her would-be rapist, his fists pounding the trapped man, more blood spattering Argernon's fists with every punch. Men rushed toward the fight from the other end of the corridor.

Casey gasped when she realized they were more Collis.

She could tell them apart easily now, including by their uniforms. The Collis also wore black, but their outfits were styled differently.

Despite being a man down, the Collis now outnumbered the Zorn ten to four.

A groan caught Casey's attention.

Speak of the devil—the Collis who had gone flying was cradling his broken arm as he tried to get up. He shook his head as if to clear it, rising to his knees.

It was the guy who had killed Rachael.

Rage hit Casey. Even though she hadn't known the woman for more than a few terrified moments, the poor woman had died in terror, trying not to be raped.

Quickly looking around, she saw the dropped tool on the floor from Argernon's man who had been working on the *conis*. It was a metal instrument with a long, thick screwdriver-type implement on one end of it.

Casey snatched up the tool and stormed toward the man struggling to get up.

She knew these aliens had boarded the Zorn ship with every intention of stealing human women and raping them. But that Collis had also said the women were worth a fortune…

After violating her body, they'd planned to sell her to the highest bidder.

Her temper flamed higher when the man turned his head and he growled at her. Their language wasn't translated by the *conis*, so she didn't know what he said—and she didn't care. His growl was vicious with intent.

He moved fast, even injured, and bounded to his feet. He snarled as he came at her.

"Fuck you!" Casey screeched as she launched herself at the alien. Their bodies slammed together and they hit the ground, the Collis taking Casey's weight.

A scream sounded.

It was *his*, not hers.

Casey felt a vibration throughout her whole body when the alien shuddered. She stared at the stunned expression on his face. Something warm slowly spread over her hands, arms, and chest where she was pressed against him. She stumbled away as the alien struggle to his knees—then she saw the gaping hole in his chest, high up between his ribs.

He looked down his body, seeing his blood pouring down his belly and groin. His head snapped up to gape at her in shock. His hands clutched at the wound but blood still ran over fingers.

"Go to hell," Casey whispered, knowing he was going to die with the heavy tool still gripped in her wet, blood-soaked hands. "That's for Rachael."

The man's eyes rolled up into his head before he fell back, his large body crashing to the floor.

Casey finally turned away. The fighting was still going on but she saw several bodies down. Anxiety gripped her as she scanned the large bodies on the floor until she realized they weren't Zorn.

She got a glimpse of Argernon when the two men fighting nearest her went to the floor together. He was still on his feet, fighting another Collis.

Argernon spun, his powerful leg shooting out, nailing the man. The Collis hit the wall hard and went down. Argernon roared his rage. She saw blood on his face briefly before the continuing melee blocked her view once more.

A sound carried from behind her and Casey spun around.

Zorn men, six of them, were running from the opposite direction. They actually had to jump over the alien she'd killed. One of the men grabbed Casey, his arm locking around her waist. She gasped as her feet left the floor and he swung her out of the center of the corridor. He leaned back against the wall and adjusted her in his tight embrace, until they were chest to chest. She dangled a good half foot from the floor but still had to raise her chin to get a look at his face.

She did an instant double-take.

The man looked a hell of a lot like Argernon—almost identical.

He sniffed at her, frowning as his gaze met Casey's. He growled softly. She waited but the *conis* didn't translate. She glanced at it on the wall, and it didn't look further damaged, but it still wasn't working.

She looked back at the man. "Can you understand me?"

He nodded briefly then turned his attention to the battle. Casey did the same.

The Zorn men had all of the Collis who were still alive on the floor. Argernon stumbled forward from the mess, covered in blood.

His head lifted. Their gazes locked.

"Let me go," she said to the man holding her.

The Zorn let her slide down his body, releasing her the second her feet touched the floor. Casey was shaking as she closed the distance to

Argernon. He just stood there waiting. She was alarmed with how pale he looked...and there was so much blood on him. He had it on his face, in his hair, down his chest, arms, and shoulders. His pants were torn above the knee on one leg. Blood even covered his bare feet.

She was in front of him in seconds. "Are you all right?"

Her hands reached out but he growled at her, showing sharp teeth.

She jerked her hands back to just stare up at him. "You look so pale. Please let me touch you."

He growled again, holding out his hands, showing her the blood as he turned his hands over. He met her gaze, slowly shaking his head. He made a sound she identified as he mimicked rushing water.

Relief hit her. "You want to shower before I touch you?"

He nodded.

The man who had grabbed Casey walked up behind her. He growled something to Argernon, causing him to smile slightly. He opened his mouth, maybe to respond, but instead of growling, he softly groaned.

Any remaining color drained from Argernon's face as he slowly sank to the floor.

Casey scrambled to catch him. He was too damn big to hold up but she did manage to slow him just enough so the man behind her could lunge forward to grab him too. The man gently lowered Argernon to the floor. Casey ended up on her knees next to him, clutching his hand. His eyes were shut, he was far too pale, and while he was still breathing, he was definitely unconscious.

Argernon's look-alike snarled loudly at the men around them. He grabbed Casey's arm, pulling her away from Argernon. She cried out in protest but the man moved fast. He dug his hands under Argernon's body, lifting him up while groaning slightly. Both men were about the same massive size, but the Zorn managed to stand with Argernon cradled in his arms.

He man snarled, jerked his head toward Casey, and then was storming away with Argernon, quickly turning out of sight.

One of the Zorn men stepped forward to grip Casey's arm. He softly growled at her as he gently pulled her to her feet, then took her hand and led her down the corridor, in the direction the other man had taken Argernon.

She walked faster, almost running. Then she *did* run when they caught sight of the man carrying Argernon. She tore her hand from her escort's hold and rushed forward, reaching Argernon just as the look-alike stopped at a door. He growled and her escort ran to catch up, putting his palm on the identification pad.

The door opened to reveal some kind of medical room. Casey saw an older Zorn man approach as Argernon was gently placed on a high, flat bed. The Zorn doctor, Casey assumed, shot her a curious glance then ignored her, quickly going to work.

Argernon's obvious relative moved to stand next to Casey. She looked up at him. "Are you Argernon's brother?"

He stared down at her, offering a nod.

"Is that a doctor?"

The man hesitated before he shook his head no.

"Where's the doctor?" Fear hit Casey. "He needs one. Isn't there a doctor on the ship?"

The man looked grim as he growled, shaking his head, clearly pissed as his eyes lingered on his brother's still form.

The man attending Argernon was cleaning off the blood. Casey moved forward to snatch up some of the small hand-sized towels the man had put on a table next to the bed. She began working on his other side, helping to wipe the blood.

Argernon's brother helped strip him out of his pants, revealing a knife wound on his thigh, inches above the knee, where one of the Collis bastards must've stabbed him. They couldn't talk to each other but both men understood when she indicated she wanted to turn Argernon onto his stomach. That was something, but she was still frustrated and filled with worry. They found a large bleeding lump on the back of his head.

He had other assorted cuts, bruises and a few claw marks to show for the fighting. The worst and most worrisome injury was his head wound. The bulge was too large for Casey's liking.

"Do you have ice? I need something very cold to put on the wound to reduce the swelling."

The older Zorn gave her the equivalent of an ice pack, which she applied, but other than cleaning, not much else could be done for Argernon's head injury. Casey and the Zorn cleaned the other wounds, bandaging larger ones. The older man might not be a doctor, but he obviously had at least a little medical training.

153

She continued to help him treat other Zorn injured in the fight against the Collis as the men found their way into the medical room.

* * * * *

At the time of the attack, they'd been three days from Zorn. It was now two days later, and while the ship was crippled, the engines were fine.

The *conis* translation program was damaged and they weren't able to fix it. Communications were down all over the ship. They couldn't even get in contact with the Zorn home planet. The Collis had taken out their long-distance communications system when they'd fired on the ship.

After a lot of frustration, Casey had managed to get a clear picture of their circumstances by asking carefully crafted yes-or-no questions. She knew some parts of the ship weren't livable, so most of the Zorn had moved to deck three, were Casey and Argernon were currently located. The water filtration systems were down, so aside from a supply kept on hand for drinking, showers were out. Casey knew they were also having problems with food, since she was given packets of dried foods to eat.

Casey continued to tend to the various Zorn men who were injured. Over twenty Collis had been killed after boarding the ship, and the Zorn had suffered four losses, as well as the death of Rachael. At least thirty Zorn males were living in the same area as Casey, and considering the water situation, pretty much everyone smelled less than pretty after day two. The air wasn't circulating particularly well, but she'd been assured they wouldn't suffocate when she'd pointed out the poor air quality. At least that was something.

Casey stayed by Argernon's side, leaving as little as possible.

He hadn't woken up.

She was frustrated and sick with worry. Argernon was healing, the knot on his head had gone down, yet he remained unconscious. She talked to him while he slept, begging him to wake, but he continued to sleep deeply. When exhaustion threatened to take her, she climbed up on the bed to curl into his side. She rarely left the room he was kept, except to use the bathroom and when she tended the other men.

Since most of the Zorn were living literally right outside the door, Casey often felt herself under their regard—which definitely made her uncomfortable. When some of them looked at her, she didn't like the interest she saw in their eyes. Argernon wasn't able to protect her, though at least she was able to relax during his brother's frequent visits.

When they finally reached the planet, the crippled ship was boarded by other Zorn. They instantly headed for Argernon, carrying something that resembled a cot with straps. Casey stayed clear while they loaded Argernon gently, checking to make sure he was secure before carrying him out the door.

One of the men stopped her when she tried to follow, and she glared up at him.

"I go where he goes. Get the hell out of my way."

Argernon's brother stepped back into the room at that moment. He growled at the man, glanced at Casey and nodded. The big man moved out of the way so Casey could rush after Argernon.

As they boarded a small shuttle, Casey's fear kicked in. Argernon was gravely injured. She was stepping onto an alien planet without his protection. Was that even safe? She didn't know.

She moved closer to his cot, gripping his limp hand.

Chapter Nine

Casey stared at the red planet around her in muted wonder. She was too exhausted and worried for anything else right now. She'd just spent three hellish days in a damaged ship with a lot of smelly Zorn men and an unconscious Argernon, with no way to communicate save for asking questions that had yes or no answers.

The shuttle ride down to the planet's surface was bumpy and crowded with the injured. After they landed, more Zorn rushed inside the cramped space to help, going for Argernon first. Casey tried to follow the men taking him away, but once more one of them moved into her path, preventing her from staying by his side.

"*Move*, damn it! I'm with him."

The man frowned but moved out of her way after sniffing her.

She ran after the stretcher and followed the men into what looked like an office building, but she quickly realized it was a medical center of some kind. Argernon was placed on a bed in a large, private room. A machine hovered above him, scanning back and forth over his body.

Casey was allowed to stay. None of the men tried to talk to her before leaving, but then, they didn't make her leave, either, so she was grateful.

Alone now, she paced, watching Argernon, her worry increasing. He hadn't woken up in three days.

She'd forcing water into him during that time by dripping it into his mouth hour after hour, but knew he still had to be dehydrated. She'd hand-bathed him twice, with his brother's help. She hadn't seen anything to indicate infection in his cuts, and Zorn seemed to heal rather quickly. Argernon's bleeding had stopped shortly after the fight. The small gash on his head had closed and was now scabbed.

It was the bump that still had her worried. It had gone down, but not enough.

The doors to the room opened and someone entered.

Casey was taken aback at seeing her first Zorn woman.

She was probably five feet ten, muscular, and she wore a tunic top with loose pants. The woman stopped to stare at Casey for a moment before walking closer. She cleared her throat.

"Hello, Earth woman. I am Scientist and Healer Ahhu."

Casey almost dropped to her knees—and would have, if she hadn't locked them tight. "You speak English. Thank God!"

"I don't speak it." The woman touched her ear. "I have the upgraded translator implant to understand your Earth language. We also have the *conis* running, so you can understand me in this room. I will get you fitted with implants soon. What is your name?"

"Casey Santhrom. How is Argernon? He hasn't woken up in three days."

The woman darted her gaze to Argernon, clearing her throat again. "He's very ill. He hit his head hard...but he will recover."

"Why isn't he awake?"

The woman moved closer, studying Casey. She sniffed and made a face. "You smell."

Anger simmered instantly in Casey. "I've been stuck in a crippled ship in tight quarters with a bunch of men for three days—without showers. What is wrong with Argernon, damn it?"

The Zorn woman growled. "There is not a need for rudeness. I was merely stating an observation. Would you like to bathe? I will see to it that you get clothing while we take care of Argis Argernon. He should be awake by the time you are clean and smelling well again."

"Lady," Casey warned. "I'm about to lose my temper, and *then* you'll know rudeness. Tell me what's wrong with Argernon!"

Ahhu stepped back, frowning. "He injured his head enough to put his body into protective hibernation."

Casey gasped. "Hibernation? Like bears?"

The woman frowned. "What is a bear?"

"Forget it. How do we wake him up?"

Casey moved to Argernon to grip his hand. Between her worry for his health, the worry she'd lived with on the ship surrounded by the other men, and the fear of what would greet her on Zorn, she was officially an emotional mess.

"You need to bathe. Your smell is offensive. We will bathe Argis Argernon."

The door opened. Three pretty women—all tall and muscular—rushed into the room, quickly advancing on Argernon. One of them actually knocked Casey out of the way, and she ended up stumbling back several feet.

The distress on the women's faces was evident as they ran their hands gently over Argernon's still body. One of them turned her attention on Ahhu.

"Will he recover?"

Ahhu nodded. "Yes, Bara. He had swelling in his brain but it has left no permanent damage. He shut down for more than a day so his body responded in kind to protect him. He's hibernating."

The woman nodded, tears filling her eyes. "We'll wake him. But only after we bathe him, so he isn't upset by his odor." She sniffed lightly. Her face scrunched in obvious distaste as she leaned closer, inhaling slowly.

Then she lifted her head, her attention going straight to Casey—and she looked really pissed off as she glared right at her.

"Who is she? Her *stench* is all over Argernon. I didn't detect it at first because of his body odor and all the other male scents."

"Who are *you*?" Casey didn't like the way the woman was glaring at her one bit. She was also ticked that three women had their hands on Argernon after pushing her out of the way. "And why in the hell are you touching him? Are you his sisters?"

Ahhu cleared her throat as she looked between both women. She softly growled. Then she turned her attention to Casey, looking really uncomfortable.

"These are Argis Argernon's house helpers. This is Bara, Valle, and Din."

Bara snarled. "Why are you addressing her? You address *me*. I am house lead."

Ahhu visibly flinched. "This is very displeasing for all of you, obviously. But...Argis Argernon bound this Earth woman, Bara. I must address her first, now. You no longer lead his house. *She* does."

Bara snarled, swaying a little on her feet. She glared at Casey.

Casey easily read the emotions in the woman's face. The woman— Bara—was furious, shocked, and, judging by the way her fingers clawed, she wanted to shred Casey to ribbons.

Casey was in shock too. Argernon had told her about house helpers. She let the information he'd given her slam into her brain as understanding hit her hard. She stared at the three women and jealousy reared its ugly head—but mostly it was pain that filled her.

These three women lived with Argernon, slept in his bed with him since he wasn't bound, and he kept them as his lovers.

Her knees shook a little. She backed up to sit down hard in the nearest chair. She felt betrayed and heartbroken. The anger and pain tore her apart. He'd said he wanted bound to her, but she'd never thought, never even considered, that he might have house helpers living with him.

Casey forced herself to her feet. She clenched her teeth as she blinked back tears to stare at the doctor, or whatever she was. "I'd like that shower. And please address," Casey's eyes went to Bara, "*her* as lead. I'm not bound to him. He's got enough damn women in his bed."

161

Casey let her gaze drift to Argernon. The women were still touching him. One had her hand on his thigh, right against his balls; another one had her hand over his heart, rubbing his bare chest as a lover would; and Bara was touching his hair.

Jealousy consumed her. She wanted to cry but she blinked the moisture back, tearing her gaze from Argernon to Ahhu.

"I want to leave now." Her voice shook, and Casey hated that her pain was evident.

Ahhu frowned, but before she could respond, the door opened and Argernon's brother from the ship strode in. He quickly took in the room—and froze in place.

Behind him, another man entered. At his side was a human woman, gripping his hand tightly. This man was obviously another brother, judging by the way he also looked so much like Argernon.

How many damn brothers were there?

"This is very tense," Ahhu said softly. She turned her attention to one of the brothers. "Argis Rever, there is a problem."

Rever frowned. "What is Argernon's condition? Will he survive?"

Ahhu hesitated as her eyes darted from Casey to the other three women. She nodded. "He will recover. His body went into hibernation from the trauma due to the head injury and…other complications. His helpers will bathe him and revive him." She paused. "He didn't tell his bound about his house helpers. She's stating she is no longer his bound, and wishes to leave now. I can smell her pain from here. She's very agitated."

162

Rever turned to Casey.

She blinked hard as she met the eyes of the man she'd spent the last three days with, glad to finally know his name.

Rever opened his mouth and then slammed it shut. He frowned at Casey, his intensely blue eyes locking on her.

"Son of a bitch," the human woman ground out, jerking away from the man holding her hand. "Your brother is an *asshole*. Damn it, this is why your people shouldn't be allowed to take Earth women! I *told* you this was going to happen." She spun around, looking at Casey, sympathy welling in those eyes. "I'm Ariel. He didn't tell you he had three women living with him?"

Casey shook her head. "I want to leave." She was proud that her voice didn't break. "Right now."

Ariel shut her eyes. When the man behind her touched her back, she jumped, startled, and spun again. "Don't touch me, damn it. This is... *Shit!*" She faced Casey again. "Did he bound you to him?"

Casey hesitated. She looked at the three women who were still rubbing and touching Argernon as he lay unconscious on the bed. Pain and anger flooded her at the same time.

Her eyes returned to Ariel. "I never signed up for this shit. Can you get me out of here? I need a shower and I need..." Her gaze flicked to Argernon. More pain hit her. She had fallen for the son of a bitch. "I need to get away from him—*and* them. Please?"

Ariel nodded. "I'm so sorry. Of course. I totally understand." She glared at the large man hovering behind her. "Let's take her home with us, Ral. Your brother is a fuck-up, and no way in hell will I let him hurt her worse. He obviously lied and kept shit from her."

Ahhu moved toward the bed to open a drawer beneath it. She took out a wand and some other, smaller device. She pointed the small device at a screen affixed to the wall, turning it on, then approached Casey.

The doctor stopped before her. "Please raise your shirt, Casey Santhrom. I need to check your lower stomach first."

"Why?" Casey took a step back.

Ariel cursed. "Just let her do it, so we can get the hell out of here."

Casey sighed, lifting her shirt. The woman waved the wand thing slowly over her stomach with one hand, then reached out and tugged at Casey's pants, lowering them to her hipbones. Finished with the wand, the woman turned her head, focusing on the green image on the screen. Casey followed her stare but didn't know what she was looking at.

Ahhu tensed. Her gaze flew back to Casey.

"You are bound to Argis Argernon, regardless of your wish not to be. You took his seed into your belly."

The three women surrounding Argernon gasped. Din and Valle looked outraged, but Bara sniffed loudly—then tears were sliding down her cheeks, her pain obvious. The woman lowered her head.

Casey frowned at the doctor. "You can't make me stay with him just because I gave him a damn blow job. How in the hell does that wand thing even know about it?"

Ariel cursed. "Oh man. That's not what they mean. They talk differently. Planting seed in your belly isn't about swallowing. That's the Zorn way of saying that you're carrying his baby. He got you pregnant, Casey."

Casey stared at Ariel in shock. "No."

Ariel stepped close to grip Casey's hand. "I'm so sorry...but if Ahhu says you been planted, then you are." She reached down to lift up her baggy shirt. "Trust me."

She stared at Ariel's obviously swollen stomach. She guessed she was at least five months pregnant.

Casey shook her head. "I don't care if I'm pregnant. I'm not living in his damn polygamist household."

"I understand," Ariel said softly. She turned, still gripping Casey's hand. "Can we take her home with us?"

Ral shook his head, looking sympathetic. "She's bound to him, Ariel. I can't interfere unless he's abusing her."

"What do you call *this*?" Ariel yelled at him. She waved her hand at Argernon and his house helpers. "You know exactly how *I'd* feel right now, damn it!" The woman tossed a dirty look at the other brother. "What in the hell was he thinking? You were with him."

Rever hesitated before saying, "I didn't even know he'd found a woman. Once his jumper from Earth docked with the ship, I didn't see him until after we were attacked. Then he was injured, so we couldn't talk. I didn't know until the first moment I saw Casey that he'd bound her. His scent was all over her—and hers on him. She cared for him during her

165

every waking minute after his injury, and slept at his side when she rested."

"I want to go home," Casey whispered. "I..." She stared into Ariel's eyes and pleaded. "I just want to go home. I want to wake up. This is a nightmare, right? I just want my life back!"

Ariel gave Casey's hand a squeeze before shooting a pleading look at the big man still hovering near her. "Do something, Ral."

The big man frowned, looking really unhappy, but he nodded. He eyed the three helpers. "Go home. She's his bound, and he failed to warn her about you. She's from a monogamous planet. Until he wakes to settle the mess he's made, it is best if she is not upset further. Your presence distresses her."

Bara she shook her head. "She knows nothing of our men! How will she revive him?"

A growl tore from Ral's mouth before he gave a curt nod to Bara. "You stay. They go." He gave his attention to Ariel next. "Trust me on this. Take his bound to get clean. I will stay here to tend to my brother until you get back." He gave a nod at Ahhu. "Show them to another room with a shower."

Ariel narrowed her eyes. "Why do you want us out of here so badly? I know you too well, Ral. Why is she talking about?" Ariel pointed at Bara.

Another growl rumbled from Ral. "Trust me—take his bound to shower. When she returns, Argernon will be awake, then he can fix this mess himself."

"But—"

"Ariel, I love you. Do as I ask. Please?"

"Damn. I hate it when you give me that look. Fine." Ariel turned to Casey. "Let's get you a shower, a change of clothes and some food. Ral's making the women go home. Argernon will wake up and then you can tear his balls off." She shot Ral a glare. "And he deserves it."

Ral gave a sharp nod. "He does. You warned him well about human women. Thank you." He gave her a wink.

"You owe me big." She shot him a reluctant smile.

Casey made herself not look at Argernon or his three live-in sex playmates. She felt betrayed and hurt. Jealousy still took up a huge chunk of her emotions, too. It burned in her as Ahhu led them out of the room.

But...she was *pregnant*? She couldn't be.

Of course, they'd had sex so much that even she had to admit it was possible.

Ariel gave a tug on her hand, leading a reeling Casey into the room next to the one Argernon was in.

Ahhu spoke to Ariel. "I'll have someone bring food and clothing for Argis Argernon's bound. I'll also start the medications we give you, so she doesn't suffer the swelling and heat that you did."

"Thanks." Ariel took a step in the path of the Zorn woman before she could escape. "Why did Ral want us out of the room?"

Ahhu swallowed hard. Her gaze darted to Casey and then back to Ariel. "Ask Argis Ral. It is not my place."

Ariel let go of Casey's hand to step closer to the Zorn woman, staring up at her. "I'm asking *you*. Don't bullshit me, Ahhu. We've gotten to know each other really well these last few months. I'd even consider you a good friend. What in the hell is Ral trying to hide? Casey deserves the truth."

Ahhu was looking really uncomfortable. "It would upset her greatly."

Casey frowned. "I'm already upset. Just spit it out. What other fucked-up thing am I not being told that's going to make me want to shoot Argernon?"

Ahhu met Casey's gaze. "Our males are different from yours. They are very sexual. When a Zorn male is seriously injured, they hibernate to slow their body functions, since they are unable to address their own needs." The woman glanced at Ariel. "His lack of release is forcing hibernation more than his injuries, at this point. To wake him fully, his body must be awoken first."

"Goddamn it!" Ariel took a step away from the door. "Ahhu, you get your ass in there and tell them to not let that woman touch him. I'm going to talk to Casey. Do you understand? If that's what he needs, *she'll* be the one to do it. Go now."

Ahhu fled.

Casey looked at Ariel with a frown. "What in the hell am I missing?"

Ariel looked murderous. "I can tell you what you *aren't* going to be missing—me yelling at my husband, because they're going to hear it clear across the other side of the planet when I see him.

Ariel sighed. "What Ahhu said, in their roundabout way of speaking, is that because Argernon couldn't get off for days, his body is in shock, and keeping him shut down. To wake him up, he needs to get his little guys moving...if you know what I mean. My husband sent us in here so muscle chick could fuck Argernon while he's down for the count, to bring him out of hibernation. That's what you'd have to do to wake him up, Casey. But maybe a hand job will do the trick."

Casey shut her eyes briefly from the pain those words caused. She felt sick.

She opened her eyes, meeting Ariel's concerned gaze.

"Let her. He doesn't belong to me. He's just a four-timing asshole, and I..." She hated the tears that filled her eyes. "I don't give a damn. Where's that shower and food? I want off this planet when Argernon wakes up, after he gets his fuck from that bitch. I'm suffering from exhaustion and I'm just...done."

Casey spun away to locate the bathroom. She slammed the door, locked it, and slid down the cool surface to the floor.

She let everything out while she cried.

Or she tried. The pain she experienced at finding out about those other women was deep.

She cried because she'd been kidnapped. She cried because she wanted her life on Earth back. She cried over the heated days she'd spent onboard with Argernon before the ship was attacked, and the days following the attack, when she'd cared for him, stayed by his side, worried over him.

Most of all, she cried because she'd fallen in love with the bastard.

169

Chapter Ten

Argernon's fingers were twisting in Casey's hair. He enjoyed the feel of her tongue, licking at the head of his cock. A growl poured out as pleasure seared through him.

Her hot tongue jerked away seconds before he was coming hard. Ecstasy made him groan loudly as his release exploded from his body.

He liked it better when Casey wrapped her mouth around him to take his seed down her throat, but he wasn't going to complain about any way that she wanted to touch him.

Opening his eyes, a lazy smile playing on his lips, he found himself staring up at a white ceiling.

It wasn't the metal ceiling on the ship. Confusion hit.

Casey tugged her hair, trying to break free of his hold.

He moved his head, feeling strangely weak—and stared in surprise at Bara, as she gave him a hate-filled glare filled with accusation. His fingers were still fisted in her hair.

"I'm not your filthy *human*," she spat. "I had to suffer hearing you moan her name over and over as I woke you!" She gave a hard tug of her head, trying once more to get him to release her.

Distress tore through Argernon. He yanked his hand away as if he'd been burned.

Bara rose to her feet as Argernon realized he was on a bed in...*medical*? His gaze flew around the room. He was on Zorn. How could it be?

Movement in the corner caught his attention. Ral was leaning against the door. His brother looked at him grimly before his attention slid to Bara.

"Thank you," Ral told her gruffly.

Bara gave a hiss of anger. "You are not welcome. He said *her* name! And you refused to leave me alone with him. I do not enjoy someone watching me with my protector."

Ral took a deep breath. "You're angry, so I did not trust you with him until you calmed. A woman in a rage is a woman I wouldn't leave alone with my defenseless brother. It is not like I haven't seen you tongue a male before."

Snarling, Bara flashed sharp fangs at Ral. Whipping her head around, she glared once more at Argernon. "You promised to protect me and give me a home. I will not release you from your word! I—"

"Leave now," Ral growled. "Give him time to recover."

Bara went stomping for the door.

Argernon sat up slightly, only then noticing he was naked. His body was damp and the scent of soap was on him. Someone had washed his hair and bathed him.

He was confused as hell as he struggled to sit up all the way and cover his cock with the sheet. Anger was evident in Ral's stiff posture as he approached.

"The ship was attacked by the Collis," Ral said. "You suffered injuries when you fought them and you have been unconscious for three days. They were going after the human women, to sell them for profit. There are some Collis willing to pay for Earth women, as forced house helpers. Somehow they heard about what the women are like, sexually."

Argernon paled, the blood draining from his face. "I remember. Casey…" Pain pierced his chest. Had she died?

"She is alive—but not well."'

Argernon rolled his body to the edge of the bed to swing his legs over. He would have gotten to his feet but Ral moved faster, grabbing him by his shoulders firmly and holding him in place. His brother shook his head.

"Do not try to get out of bed. You are weak and unsteady. Ahhu had to hook you up for nourishment. You need some hours for your body to recover, since you just came out of hibernation. You would be in much worse shape, but your Casey forced nutrient paste and water down your throat for three days as she tended to you."

"Where is she? If she is hurt, I need to be with her! Were we attacked by more Collis? Take me to her. If I can't walk then by the Lord of the Moons, carry me to her side! I bound her."

"I know what you've done."

Argernon frowned. "Your rage is so strong I can almost taste it, brother. Why?"

"Ariel is angry with me. She screamed at me and beat my chest with her fists. She is carrying my offspring, and upsetting her is bad for her health! The only reason I don't beat on you in turn is because you are already weak. Ariel won't even speak to me. She's that angry."

"I don't have time to figure out why Ariel is angry with you. *Where is Casey?* If I can't go to her then can she come to me? I want to see her myself, to make sure she is well."

"She's alive." Ral took a deep breath. "She won't see you, brother. She is currently barricaded in the next medical room and refuses to speak to anyone at all. Ariel has ordered us to leave your bound woman alone until she calms down. My belly-swollen bound is sitting in the hallway, trying to talk Casey into speaking again." Ral growled. "You really made a mess."

Argernon frowned. "Casey is…" He shook his head. "What is going on?"

"You didn't tell her you had house helpers! The three of them rushed to your side when you were brought to the medical building. Casey was at your side already. Ahhu said it was tense and painful for all of them as the women met. Bara was unpleasant to your bound, and I'm sure Ahhu was putting it mildly."

"Lord of the Moons," Argernon groaned.

"Rever, Ariel and I walked into that. Your house helpers were rubbing your body and touching you. Your bound was as white as a moon fish and

173

I could smell her pain the instant I entered. Ariel took in the situation and reacted like she always does when she is very angry. Casey renounced you as her bound."

Argernon growled, trying to climb off the bed again. "No! I won't let her go."

"Stay put," Ral snarled back. "Ahhu has taken care of it already. Casey can't renounce you."

Argernon stared at his brother. "I don't understand."

Ral took a deep breath. "Ahhu checked your Casey over. Good planting, brother. You got your bound with offspring."

Argernon mouth dropped open before a grin stretched his face. "You are sure?"

Ral took a step back, crossing his arms over his chest. "Positive. We were all in the room, including your three helpers. Though I don't know what you are grinning over." Ral's eyes narrowed. "Your bound hates you and thinks you are the biggest deceiver on Zorn. She knows that Bara just woke you up from hibernation—and how that was done."

Argernon paled. "She knows that Bara tongued me?"

Ral gave a grim nod. "Yes."

"But I didn't have a say—"

Ral sighed. "It doesn't matter to them. Trust me. If another woman touched me, Ariel would remove a body part." His hand slid down his body to cup his balls.

"Why did you let her?" Argernon snarled. "You were in the room!"

"You had to be woken from hibernation. Do you think your bound would touch you after watching three of your house helpers rub their hands all over your body? Three helpers you made no arrangements to find other homes for, so they were gone by the time you arrived back on Zorn?" Ral growled. "You didn't even warn her that you had them under your protection. When I brought Ariel to my home, I sent my helpers away before we arrived. What were you thinking? You were warned by my Ariel that human women are monogamous."

"I was going to," Argernon snarled. "I had time still to make arrangements. Casey wasn't sure she wanted bound to me. I had bound her already but she asked for time to decide, and I wanted her willing to be my bound. I..." He shook his head. "I must speak to her."

"It may be hopeless," Ral said. "She may not forgive you. Ariel has warned me of this. You have wounded your bound. She had tears—and a lot of them, from the sound of it. You hurt her very deeply. Human women are not like Zorn, Argernon. If you hurt one deeply, they refuse to let you into their heart...and without capturing their hearts, they will never allow themselves to be bound to you. You should have told her about your women, and made sure she didn't have to see them touching you."

"I told her about house helpers."

"Did you tell her that you had three of them?"

Argernon shook his head. "I was going to tell her that I would find them other homes, and that by the time we reached Zorn, they would be out of my life so she would be my only woman. The alarms sounded as I started to share with her my plans for the two of us.

"She carries my seed in her belly, Ral. She means everything to me. I understand now why you feel as you do for Ariel. I understand how you could give up your helpers for one woman. How do I fix this and get her back? I will *not* lose her."

Ral reached out to clasp his brother's arm. Sympathy welled in his eyes. "I do not know."

"I have to get her back. I have to make this right." Agony hit Argernon at the thought of losing Casey forever.

Casey realized she was being childish. She'd barricaded the door with the bed and a desk. Guilt hit her over the pregnant Ariel in the hallway, who kept trying to coax her into opening up. She reluctantly admitted that she could have handled this better.

She moved for the door. "Ariel?"

"I'm here."

"Are you alone? If I open the door, will you come in alone?"

"I promise."

Sighing, Casey moved everything away from the door to unlock it. She peered into the hallway to see Ariel smiling at her, alone as promised.

"No one is here but me. I sent everyone away. Can we talk?"

Casey let her in but she locked the door behind them. "I'm sorry. I took this really bad."

"I don't blame you." Ariel sat down in a chair. She massaged her belly absently. "I'd be upset too. Argernon really screwed up."

"He should have told me."

"Yes. And he should have sent them away. He knew that if he bound one of us, he'd have to give up other women. I told him how our species is."

"It hurts. I thought he cared about me, and I thought I was special to him. I fell for the asshole," Casey admitted softly. "At first I was pissed when I realized he wasn't returning me to Earth. When he first kidnapped me, I—"

"He what?"

Casey explained how she met Argernon, how she'd ended up aboard the jumper, and some of the details of her time with him before the Collis arrived. "Then we were attacked, and I thought he was going to die. I stayed at his side on that damn small bed for three days, praying he'd live so I could tell him that I love him. I was such a damn idiot. I should have known. We're from two different worlds apart, literally, and it's not like I really got to know him. How in the hell could I have fallen for someone so damn hard and so damn fast anyway?"

"I understand. I fell for Ral like that. I fell the first time he made love to me, I swear. He was amazing. He was so protective and masculine, and he comforted me. I was kidnapped by a race of these lizard people and Ral fought a bunch of other Zorn men to win me."

"Wow."

Ariel smiled. "Not that we haven't had our ups and downs, we have, but I love him. He's like breathing air to me—I need him that badly. He'll do anything to make me happy, and he makes sure I know how much he loves me."

Sadness settled in Casey. "Argernon said he'd make me happy."

"They're different from human guys, but with Ral, I find that's a wonderful thing. I'm so sorry, Casey. Maybe he was going to send them to another household. You could just ask him."

She shook her head. "Let him talk to Bara or Din or Valle. He's got plenty to choose from."

"They have a high sex drive. I can attest to that. Zorn men are walking hard-ons." A grin split Ariel's lips. "That has its advantages. Trust me. My sex life is over the top, and it never gets boring or old or slows down." She rubbed her stomach. "I was afraid Ral would lose interest in me when I got a big belly, but he thinks I'm even sexier the bigger I get. The man has me totally addicted to having sex every few hours of every day." Ariel eyed Casey. "It's not just a culture thing for Argernon to have three women in his household. It's a physical necessity."

"So I've heard. I still think he's a male slut."

"He's second in line to rule this entire planet. He's like a prince. I've learned a lot since coming to Zorn. I thought women were mistreated and kind of had slave status when I first came here, but that's not true. Women have a hell of a lot more say and control over their lives than you'd think. They're raised without jealousy of other Zorn women sharing a household. Their bodies can't handle sex as much as the men need it, so

178

according to the Zorn women I've spoken to, they like having other women to share that burden." Ariel snorted. "They call being oversexed a burden. I don't think they enjoy it as much as we do."

"That bites for them."

Ariel chuckled. "Totally. Zorn women only get jealous of bound women, because they're the men's favored women, the ones who will have his children and are in charge of the households. A lot of women are willing to give that up to be house helpers, though, because being in a good home means power and prestige to them."

"How does cleaning someone's house and being a bed warmer amount to powerful and prestigious?"

"I'm with you there, but think about all the women who marry rich guys for their money. It's the same here in that way. All Zorn women could bound to Zorn men if they wanted to, but the truth is that most of them would rather live in a house with one or two other women, if the man has the equivalent of money here. They get the best houses, the best food…the best of everything. But they share all household duties with other women."

Casey eyed Ariel with a frown. "Do you have house helpers at your place? Do you let Ral touch other women? I won't judge or anything. I hope I'm not being too nosey. I just can't see myself ever living that way and being happy. Are you?"

Another chuckle escaped Ariel. "We have a helper. I'm thrilled she's there. She's an older woman, much older, and she treats me like the daughter she always wanted. As far as loyalty, well…if Ral touched another woman, I'd castrate him." She winked. "Not that he would. I can't get enough of him. He's got no reason to stray."

"Did he have helpers when you came here?"

"He had two, but he'd sent them to one of his brothers' houses before we landed. His father sent one to our house after I arrived though. She actually stripped naked and went on her hands and knees, shoving her ass in the air, waiting for my husband to mount her. I was *so* upset. We couldn't communicate because the damn translators couldn't read English yet. It was seriously frustrating. Try using hand signals to tell a guy if he mounts the bitch on the floor shoving her ass at him that you'd never let him touch you again." Ariel snorted. "It was hell, and I stormed out. He chased me down and he never touched her."

Casey sighed. "I can't believe I'm having his baby. My life is so fucked up."

Ariel gave her a pleading look. "Talk to him, Casey. Put your foot down by telling him what you need. He could have returned you to Earth. Hell, he didn't have to take you to begin with. If his father finds out he took you against your will, he's in deep shit. He broke the law to bring you here."

Casey was stunned. "What?"

"All human women have to bound willingly. It's against the law to kidnap an unwilling woman and bring her to Zorn. He took you and bound you without giving you a choice, Casey. If you want to hang him by his balls, all you have to do is tell his father what he did."

"Would his father send me back to Earth?"

Ariel's gaze dropped to Casey's stomach. "No. I won't lie to you." Ariel looked up. "I can't see their father letting you take off with his grandchild...and hell, your baby wouldn't be safe on Earth. You know that. When I found out I was pregnant, I realized that no matter whatever happens with Ral, I can't ever go home again. My child would be a freak. What hospital in the world could I even go to? Can you say 'media frenzy', everyone trying to use my kid as a step to fame or as a science experiment?" She rubbed her stomach. "Here on Zorn, my child will be treated just like everyone else's. They don't care that I'm human or that my child will be part human. They know about other races on other planets, and they accept them. They're peaceful, for the most part. Just being part Zorn makes my child fully accepted in their culture."

"So what am I supposed to do? Go home with Argernon and watch him fuck those three women? Maybe I can draw straws to decide who gets him in what time slot." Casey hated the bitter bite in her voice. "I hear since I'm the bound one, I get to sleep in the bed and not on the floor. Woo-hoo. Lucky me."

Ariel shook her head. "No. You set that son of a bitch straight. Tell him it's just you, or you'll find another man. Let me clue you in here— we're the hottest damn commodity on this planet. There are thousands of good men on Zorn who'd jump through every hoop you put up if you agreed to bound with one of them. They'd be loyal and never mistreat you."

"Bara did something to him to wake him up."

Ariel sighed. "I know. I was the one who had to relay your message to Ahhu after I'd sent her to stop that from happening."

"I can't forget that. I'm sorry now that I let her touch him, but I can't forget it."

Ariel nodded. "Let me talk to Ral. He knows a lot of good men. But make no mistake—you *need* to find one to protect you. I'll make Ral take you home with us and we'll introduce you to every man my husband knows, until you meet one you can fall for. We'll get you bound to someone who can make you happy and keep you safe. You need that now. Think of your baby."

Casey looked down at her stomach. "Will Argernon let his child go?"

Ariel rose to her feet. "You were forced to leave Earth and he bound you without consent, since you were clueless about what it meant when he came inside you. He broke the law. If push comes to shove, he won't have a damn choice. As long as the baby is on Zorn, and is safe, I don't see how his father can protest. Hyvin Berrr could still see his grandchild, no matter what man raises him. There are a lot of great Zorn men, Casey. You could be happy here."

It broke her heart, but Casey nodded. "I can't be with Argernon again. I can't let him hurt me more than he already has."

"Let me go speak to Ral, and then we'll go home. I'm so damn sorry, Casey. Argernon was a real asshole, and I hope he suffers for what he's done to you."

Casey watched the woman walk away, her shoulders slumped. For all she knew, Bara was fucking Argernon right now.

Just the thought of it made her hurt worse.

Chapter Eleven

Casey's ears no longer bothered her. Before she'd left the medical building, Ahhu had given her a shot so she could painlessly put two implants in them. Casey could understand anyone talking to her now, but she'd been warned that not all Zorn could understand *her*. The English program was new, and unless a Zorn thought they would be dealing with humans, not all of them took the time to upgrade their implant programs for translation.

It was late at night and Casey was exhausted. It had taken hours for Ahhu to find the time to implant the translators into her ears. Ral had begged Ariel to go home with him because she was pregnant, arguing that she needed her rest, and Ariel had given in after making it clear that Casey would be transported to their home when Ahhu was done with the procedure.

Three large Zorn males escorted Casey from the medical building to a waiting vehicle, driving her to a large, beautiful house on a hill. Zorn homes weren't like Earth houses. They were more rounded, single story, and made out of some material Casey had never seen before that looked like sheets of stone. The men escorted her to the door and one of them placed his palm on a scanner while smiling down at Casey.

"You are home. I am to escort you inside to your room. Would you like me to wake someone to bring you food?"

"I just want to sleep. It's late, so I don't want to disturb Ariel or her husband."

The man nodded as he opened the door. "This way."

The other two men stayed outside. Casey walked into a large living room with an open floor plan. The lights were dimmed, but still bright enough to see by. Two couches, some tables and some rugs decorated the room. The furniture looked like wood, but it was a dark red that starkly contrasted with the utter whiteness of the floor and walls. It was a nice home.

The man led her down a hallway. All doors were shut except to the room on the end. He walked in and waved his hand along the wall to turn on the lights in the bedroom.

"There is a sensor here. Wave your hand to turn the light on or off." He indicated to an open door across the room. "This room is for your personal needs. Wave your hand high to turn on the water. There are motion sensors that control the water flow." When she nodded, he backed out of the room. "Good living, human." He smiled before striding away.

Casey sighed as she softly shut the door. She didn't want to disturb her hosts. Ariel *had* been exhausted when her husband had led her away. Casey felt guilty about that, though she'd been very grateful for Ariel's friendship. The woman was just as outraged as Casey had been about what Argernon had done. It made her feel better to know one person who understood.

She turned her attention the room, taking in the bed, a massive four-poster that was high off the floor. All the Zorn men were well over six feet tall, while the women she'd seen were around five-ten and up, making them taller than the average human. Even their bodies were larger than most humans, with their muscles and bigger bone structures. Casey felt small for once in her life, almost fragile compared to the people she now lived with.

To each side of the bed were tables with drawers. A dresser-like piece of furniture took up one entire low wall, under a large window. She walked over to look out. Nothing covered the window, so she stared out into utter darkness that gave her the creeps. Someone could be out there, watching her right back, and she wouldn't know it. She looked up, but there were no marks on the wall to indicate curtains or blinds had ever hung there. Maybe Zorn people didn't believe in curtains. It made her feel like a fish in a bowl.

She ignored the bathroom for now. She'd used the one at the medical center before she'd left. They'd even given her a weird-looking toothbrush. She placed a bag down by the bed. It had some personal items the medical center had given her, including medication she was supposed to take every day. Since she was pregnant, Ahhu had warned that her body temperature would rise without the medication, since Zorn ran hotter than humans. The meds would also help avoid swelling from her body thinking it needed to retain fluids, another symptom she'd face as a human pregnant by a Zorn.

Casey kicked off the boots they'd given her. Reaching for her waist, she unfastened her pants, kicking them off. She decided to just sleep in a shirt. She wished that Zorn had bras and underwear, but Ariel had already told her they didn't make them for women. Zorn women rarely wore clothing at home. They hated anything tight against their bodies.

She eyed the room again before waving off the lights, then found the bed and had to climb into it, literally, since it was so high.

She was physically and mentally exhausted—and she *hated* that she thought about Argernon, but she couldn't stop.

He was awake and he was going to be fine. He'd wanted to talk to her. He'd asked Ahhu to give her a message. He'd wanted her to know that he'd never meant to keep the other women after he'd bound her, and asked if she would please see him.

She didn't want to talk to him. And she sure didn't want to see him. She was done being hurt. What kind of man just tossed aside three women who depended on him, anyway? Her opinion of Argernon was in the toilet, no matter how her heart felt.

As she curled on her side on the comfortable bed, she wondered if Argernon was still at the medical building…or if maybe he was currently snuggled up in his own bed with his three lovers.

It hurt Casey to picture it. She utterly despised the jealousy that caused her so much pain. She told herself yet again that she was better off without him, even as her hand slid down to curl over her stomach through the thin shirt she wore to bed.

Argernon's baby rested inside her.

The shock hadn't worn off yet.

Casey couldn't deny that kids had always been a dream of hers. She'd of course pictured a wedding first, some nice guy who worked a nine-to-five job as her husband, and the excitement of painting a baby's room. She might have cried over that lost fantasy, but she was out of tears at the moment.

Instead, she was having an alien's baby, one who had too many damn women in his life, and she was on a planet where she'd have to hook up with a stranger to even have a house to *put* her baby in when it was born. She didn't even want to think about that right now.

Of course her mind wasn't listening to her. She'd have to find a Zorn man to marry. To bound to. It seemed like a job interview, to her mind. She'd interview men for the position, telling them what she wanted in a man, what she needed, and then have to go through the candidates to see who best could fill the role. The whole idea bit the big one.

Depression swamped her. She couldn't return to Earth with a Zorn baby—and no way in hell was she *not* having the baby. She wanted it, even if the baby's father was a lying asshole.

Rolling over, Casey blindly stared up at the ceiling. Then her head turned to the large window, but it was still too dark out there to see anything, even after her eyes had adjusted to lights off. Zorn had three moons but it was a very cloudy night so they weren't visible. Ariel had promised her a terrific view when the weather was better. It didn't matter.

Casey shut her eyes. She needed rest. She'd deal with all of this shit tomorrow, when she wasn't so wrung out.

A door slammed somewhere in the house. Guilt hit her. She must have woken someone when she'd come in, no matter how quiet she and the escort had been. She listened, but when the house remained silent, she relaxed again. She took slow, deep breaths, trying to convince her restless brain to drift off to sleep. It was the best thing for her, or tomorrow she'd be so exhausted her brain might not function at all.

Something out in the hall made a noise. Casey tensed briefly but figured it was probably Ariel's husband, getting his pregnant mate something from the kitchen. Or maybe he was making sure the doors were locked—

She gasped as the bedroom door was suddenly thrust open. Light from the hallway blinded her momentarily as she jerked upright.

Argernon stood in the doorway, the lights behind him casting his face into shadow.

Dread slammed into Casey at the sight of him.

"Welcome home, Beautiful," he growled softly to her, his voice incredibly husky. "I'm sorry for the measures I went to just to get you here. I know you don't want to see me—but I want to see *you*."

Casey was speechless as she stared back at him. He was shirtless, his hair loose and running down his chest and arms. He gripped the doorway for long seconds before slowly entering the room. He waved his hand along the wall to trigger the lights, and then again so they dimmed enough that the room was shadowed, though she could still see him perfectly.

His glowing blue eyes were fixed on her.

"Did you really think I'd let you go, Casey? Did you really think that I would keep other women when I had *you*? I was going to make arrangements for the three of them to go elsewhere, as soon as you agreed to bound with me. I thought I had time to do so; they would have been gone by the time we reached Zorn. But then the Collis..." His eyes closed briefly before he took another step. "You are the only woman who belongs in my bed, and you are the only one who will be there from now on. In fact, you look perfect in it."

She looked at the bed she sat on, confused. *His* bed...?

Understanding hit her like a physical blow. *His* bed...*his* home.

Her gaze jerked back up and suddenly he was closer. He put his hands on the end of mattress. Blue eyes stared at her intensely.

"You are everything to me, Casey. You carry my offspring in your belly. You belong to me, and we both know it. Our offspring knows it. I apologize, and I deeply regret the shock you suffered because I was unable to prepare a home that you would have welcomed happily, but I have fixed that. The helpers are gone. I have already arranged for an older house helper to come in the morning. Her duties will never include touching me. She will take care of our home and our meals. She will keep you company and be your companion. All I require is you."

Casey could actually feel her anger building, and not slowly. "You think it's that simple?"

He nodded. "I bound you, and my seed has planted in your body. I am thrilled, my Casey. Lord of the Moons, you make me so proud."

"That was so the wrong word to use."

He frowned. "What word?"

"Proud. Let me tell you what I think of *you*. You should be ashamed of yourself—and I think you're lower than a pile of dog shit."

His frown deepened. "I know ashamed, and I apologize. I made mistakes but I corrected them. I know shit, but I do not know what a dog is." His eyes narrowed. "I still understand the insult. I understand that you are angry with me."

"Understand this—I'm not bound to you. As a matter of fact, Ariel is going to introduce me to other men. I'm going to find a nice Zorn who isn't a lying asshole for me to bound to. I'm not your *anything* but the woman who happens to be carrying your child." She gave him her best death glare. "I can't believe you had those guards bring me here, knowing I want nothing to do with you!"

Rage hit Argernon's features. He snarled. His hand fisted on the bedding. "You will not bound to another male. You are *mine*."

"No. Bara, Ville and Din are yours."

"Not anymore. They're gone."

"Well, you'd better get them back, because I'm not staying here." She climbed off the mattress but she had to get closer to him to reach her pants. She grabbed them up and backed away from him. "I want to be taken to Ariel's home, where I'm supposed to be. Right now."

Hands grabbed Casey and she gasped when Argernon lifted her. She ended up sprawled flat on her back on the large bed. The pants went flying somewhere on the floor again. He pinned her to the bed under his large body, but he was careful not to hurt or crush her. His eyes were inches above hers as they glared at each other.

"You live here with *me*, in our home. You are going nowhere."

"You can't keep me here against my will!"

"I can. If you let another male touch you, I will kill him. If you escape and bound yourself to another male, he will still die, Casey. I will challenge him and kill him while you watch! You are my bound—*I won't let you go*."

Rage hit her. "You son of a bitch! Get the hell off me. You make me sick!"

He moved fast, rolling them both easily with his strength and scooping her into his arms as he slid off the bed. He carried her to the bathroom and very gently put her down. He waved his hand so the light came on. Concern etched his features as he tried to urge her toward the toilet.

"You are ill? Should I contact Ahhu? She cares for our family, and she will now care for you if you need medical attention."

Casey backed away from him. "I'm not going to puke. It's a *saying*, Argernon! It means I can't stand you, and you make me feel nauseous just looking at you. I don't need a doctor. I need you to get the hell away from me and never come near me again!"

Argernon paled. "I have made things right, Beautiful. You should know this now. You should know how committed I am to you."

"Don't call me that. Never call me that again, you son of a bitch. We're over. Do you *get* that? You're nothing but a four-timing asshole. You had three women who depended on you, who you slept with, yet you still fucked *me*. Do you think I believe you're a *better* person now, just because you shoved them to the curb for me? It just makes you a heartless bastard."

He stared at her. He looked confused.

"What don't you understand? Your girlfriends lived here and you just dumped them out like garbage. Is that supposed to make me think you're wonderful? What about when you meet someone else, and you come home to toss *my* ass out on the street? You're really a winner, Argernon. That's sarcasm, by the way, which means the opposite of truth. I think you're an asshole, and I think you're mean. I also think you should get the hell out of my way, because I want to leave."

"I didn't dump them on the street like garbage. I found them safe homes—homes they, themselves, requested to go to—when I told them I only wished to be with my bound. They are in good homes, with honorable men they wanted to be with. And I would *never* replace you. You aren't a house helper. You are my bound. I would never throw you out of our home. I swear to stay with you until death."

Some of her anger slipped away. But she shook her head sadly. "I don't want a man like you, Argernon. I just want to be free of you. I could never be with a man who lies to me and then does something shitty to someone else, three of them in fact, claiming he's doing it for my benefit. Thanks but no thanks."

"So you want me to bring them back here with us?" He frowned.

"There is no *us*. It's over, Argernon. I'm leaving. Have a nice life." She tried to walk around him.

He stepped in her path to growl softly at her. "We were happy before, Casey. Remember? It's just us again. Just you and I. Please forgive me. I made mistakes but I corrected them. If I hadn't been injured, I would have made all the arrangements before we reached Zorn. They would have been gone from your sight."

She stared up at him. He really thought it was that easy. "You lied to me. I was happy with you because I didn't know you had three other women you were fucking, waiting for you at home. One of which, I know for a fact, just fucked you hours ago. Get the hell out of my way before I *do* puke all over you. You make me sick."

He snarled. "I wasn't offered a choice. If I had been, I wouldn't have let Bara near me. I woke up with her touching me. I thought it was you. I *dreamed* it was you. It was *your* name that was the first word I spoke upon awakening."

She stared at him, more pain filling her. "It doesn't change what happened, does it? Get out of my way, Argernon. I'm leaving. Get your girlfriends back and forget we ever met. I'm certainly going to do whatever it takes to forget all about you."

Argernon's eyes narrowed. He shook his head. "No."

"You don't have a choice."

His lips curved in a wicked grin. "I *do* have choices. I won't let you go. I kidnapped you from your planet because I wanted you for my own—and I am going to keep you."

Uneasiness settled in the pit of Casey's stomach as she stared up at Argernon. "Please move."

He backed up into the bedroom. Casey followed. She snatched up the pants that had fallen from her fingers when Argernon had grabbed her earlier and stepped into them. She pulled them up, keeping her back to Argernon, and fastened them before putting on her boots. She was leaving. The bastard couldn't stop her.

She straightened and turned. Argernon was by the nightstand.

He eyed her. She eyed him back.

"Goodbye, Argernon."

For a big man, he could move fast.

He grabbed Casey around her waist. She screamed out as her boots left the floor.

She landed on the bed face first. Déjà vu hit her when she felt him pin her down with his knee while tugging her hands. This time, though, he didn't jerk them behind her back. He yanked them above her head.

She heard chains rattle.

"Don't," she yelled. "Damn it!"

A restraint closed around one wrist, then the other. His knee moved away.

Rolling over, she glared at Argernon. "You can't do this!"

He smiled but his eyes were cold. "You give me no choice." He pulled her up the bed, closer to the headboard, and then he reached for the nightstand.

Struggling didn't do a damn thing. She heard a drawer open and then Argernon used another set of restraints to secure her wrist cuffs to the headboard. She glared at him as he moved back on his knees on the bed. She kicked at him but he grabbed each of her feet in turn, tearing off her boots.

"Don't do this, Argernon. I don't want you." Tears filled her eyes. "You swore you'd never force me."

He met her eyes. "I *would* never force you. But I can't let you go, Casey. You belong to me. You're my bound." He reached down for the front of his pants and slowly stripped them off.

He was aroused. Argernon was *always* aroused. Her gaze had instantly gone to his cock, which was standing straight up. She forced herself to look away. He met her angry glare as he sat back on his legs.

"I need release. I'm in pain."

"Fuck yourself."

He nodded. "I assumed you wouldn't help."

He turned his body to stretch for the nightstand again. Another drawer opened. He withdrew a tube, which she guessed was Zorn's version of lubricant, and he confirmed it when he removed the cap, squeezing a white cream into his hand. Spreading it on his hard cock, Argernon met her angry gaze.

She refused to look down at his body again but she could still clearly see his hand moving. He didn't look away from her as he masturbated. She saw his eyes narrow and his mouth tensed. The bed moved with him as he started to pump his hips in rhythm with the fist working his shaft. She watched him tip his head back, his eyes closing, his lips parting...

He groaned as he came.

Without a word, he moved off the bed to walk into the bathroom.

Casey shut her eyes. She was in hell. He wasn't letting her go.

In the morning, Ariel *had* to come for her. She'd figure out when she woke up that something had happened. Ariel had sworn she would help her, and Casey trusted her. She just needed to get through one night with Argernon.

The water in the bathroom shut off. She opened her eyes to watch Argernon walk out of the smaller room totally naked, his glowing gaze on her.

He reached for her shirt when he settled on the bed. She tried to turn away but the annoying alien was too strong. Her shirt lifted easily as he tugged it to her ribs. His eyes went to her stomach, as did one gentle hand.

"My seed planted there," he said, his face awed.

Her heart broke all over again. "Let me go."

Beautiful blue eyes turned fierce. "Never."

He released her shirt...then both hands went for the waist of her pants to unfasten them.

She struggled, but again she was no match for Argernon. He tore her pants down her legs, leaving her bare. One of his large hands caressed her thigh. She rolled away, which left her ass exposed. He cupped her ass gently, massaging.

"Don't touch me." She turned her head to glare over her shoulder at him.

Argernon sighed. "I would never hurt you."

"You already have, more than you'll ever know. I won't forgive you. Don't you understand that? Every time you touch me, all I can see is Bara touching *you*, Din with her damn hands on your chest, Valle doing the same."

He snarled. His gaze jerked to hers. "I wasn't awake to stop them."

"They lived with you. You had sex with them. Don't act all innocent. It's not something they haven't done a thousand damn times before, Argernon."

He growled.

"And don't growl at me. I don't have three men at home who I sleep with. I don't cheat. I've never screwed around on a man in my life."

"Cheat?"

"Betray their trust by sleeping with other people when they think they're the only one."

He frowned. "House helpers don't feel betrayed if I touch other women. It is acceptable to them."

"I'm not a damn house helper!"

"You feel I betrayed you."

"I don't 'feel' shit. You *did* betray me, it's a fact. If I'd known you had those women at home waiting for you, I never would have let you touch me. The second I found out, I walked away. Not telling me something important like that is just as bad as lying. I thought I meant something to you. I thought..." She forced herself to look away from him before she started to cry, shutting her eyes tightly.

"I smell your pain." His voice lowered to a husky tone.

She ignored him.

He growled quietly. The bed moved when he stretched out next to her. "I never meant to hurt you. It hurts me that you suffer." His voice was soft. "I never planned on taking a woman from Earth, Casey. I made no arrangements like the other men did, to find homes for their house helpers. But I knew you were mine the moment I saw you in your forest, and I had to bound you. I would have found my house helpers new homes before we arrived on Zorn, if I hadn't been harmed by the Collis. I never would have let them touch me after spending my seed in you. I know you are a race that feels rage at the thought of such a thing, just as I feel rage at the thought of a male touching you. I *do* understand. Please look at me."

"No."

He took deep breaths. "I would want to kill any male if I had to watch him touch you. I want to kill at the very *thought* of another man in bed with you, inside you." He growled. "I feel pure rage at the idea of all the males who touched you before me. I *understand*, Casey."

199

"You don't." She turned her head, opening her eyes. She had to blink back her tears so she could see him. "I don't feel rage—I feel raw pain. Rage is easier to take compared to my heart feeling as if it was torn from my chest. All I can see is those women touching you, Bara fucking you. Please, if you care for me at all, get away from me."

Chapter Twelve

Argernon looked frustrated as he stared at Casey. "I swear to you that she did not mount me."

"She touched you. She got you off somehow, right?"

His eyes darkened. "I was in a dream state, and wasn't aware of what was real and what was not. I thought it was *you*, Casey. I thought it was *your* hair I had in my hand. I thought it was your breath touching me. I thought it was your tongue bringing me to release."

She stared into his eyes. She hated him and she loved him. His lifestyle caused her pain. Part of her brain reminded her that she could have prevented Bara from touching him. Casey had told Ariel to let Bara do it. She hadn't even meant it at the time, but she'd been so filled with pain and jealousy, and it was done now. She held part responsibility for that. She knew it. It didn't ease the pain, though.

"I can't get past this, Argernon. I hurt too much. I feel betrayed by you. I have pride. Do you understand? You kept important things from me that I walked into blind and it *hurt*. I don't think much of a man who makes a commitment to three women and then just dumps them when someone else comes along that he likes better."

"I don't like you better."

Casey was pretty sure her whole body flinched. She looked away from him.

Wow, had he set *her* straight.

"I love you."

Whipping her head back around, surprise overwhelmed her when she saw the sincerity burning in the depths of his eyes. He nodded slowly.

"I love you, Casey. You are everything to me. I will not lose you. You speak of pride...so let me tell you of *my* pride, and the ways I have set it aside for you. I never thought I'd hand women over to someone else to protect. I offered them a home and I thought I would never send them away. I did that because I would rather lose honor with these women than lose *you*. I would rather hurt the feelings of three women I had promised to protect because I would do anything to not hurt you even a little. You do not want me, and yet, even knowing this, I am still prepared to plead with you to forgive me and not leave me."

Casey couldn't speak. She didn't know what to say. Argernon didn't have that problem.

His mouth hardened into a tight line for a moment. "I plead for nothing." His voice deepened. "I beg for nothing." He paused, searching her eyes. "But you are my heart. I beg you to forgive me, Beautiful. You come before everything to me. You even come before my own pride. I'm a Zorn warrior. I have fought many battles. I carry scars from lives I took in those battles. I hunt and I do it well. I have never been captured and I have never been brought to my knees." He reached out to caress her cheek. "Then I look into your eyes and remember your laugh. I am there, Beautiful. You have caught me...and I am on my knees for you."

Her heart melted. How could it not? The things he was saying to her were too much. She saw honesty burning in his intense stare. His tone sent shivers down her spine. The urge to touch him was so strong that she even tried to, until her arms jerked when she moved. They stayed above her head where they were chained.

"I don't know how to get past the pain," she admitted softly. "I do love you too. I just..." She blinked back tears. "I don't know what to think about this."

He blinked. "Don't think. Feel."

"That's the damn problem. I feel hurt." Her voice broke.

"Casey," he growled, moving closer. "Let me touch you. Let me make you forget everything but us together. There's no pain in my arms or in my touch." He was so close to her mouth that she inhaled his breath. "Let me love you."

Shaking her head, she turned her face away. "No." She rolled onto her back to put a little distance between them.

Argernon sighed. "I can make you want me."

"Don't, Argernon."

"I want you and I need you. I hurt *for* you and *with* you. The thought of losing you is one I will not accept." He sat up to straddle her thighs.

Casey stared up at the naked man who was reaching for her shirt. She struggled but he had her pinned from the waist down. The restraints held her arms locked above her head.

"Damn it, Argernon. Don't do this. I won't forgive you."

"You said you can't forgive me as it is. Will this be any more unforgivable than the rest of what I have done?"

"There will be less to forgive if you don't do this on top of everything else."

He had the nerve to chuckle as he tore open her shirt. His gaze moved down her body. The smile died. "You are so sexy. Your skin is so pale. Your breasts are perfect and I love the taste of them." He dipped his head.

Casey tried to twist away but she couldn't escape his hot mouth that found one of her nipples. His hands spread wide on her stomach, holding her down, while he sucked and licked at her hardening bud. She tried to ignore the intensely amazing feeling. Argernon sucked harder. She felt it all the way down to her clit.

Squeezing her eyes shut, she bit her lip.

Argernon growled. He tore his mouth from her breast to scoot down her body, changing positions so he could push her thighs apart. Casey tried to kick him away but Argernon was faster and stronger.

He growled as he lifted his head. "Behave or I will restrain you more. I don't want to risk hurting you."

Her gaze flew to the ceiling. His gaze followed and he chuckled again. She glared at him when he had the nerve to wink.

"There is nothing there to suspend you from but I will fix that tomorrow. Tonight, I can spread your legs and bind them to the bed."

"Let me go."

He nodded. "For now." He released her thighs to back down the bed and climb off.

Casey closed her legs, glaring at him as he walked toward the dresser. He bent, showing off his muscular backside. He had the best ass ever but she didn't want to admit that, even though she was admiring it.

When he straightened, dread hit her as she saw he held long lengths of material. She swallowed as he walked to the bed with intent in his hungry eyes.

"What do you have? What are you going to do with those?"

He didn't answer. Instead, he crouched by the side of the bed. He was up to something—and she knew she wasn't going to like it. Chewing on her lip, Casey silently watched him. He was going to seduce her...and damn him, he could do it. Her body was already turned on.

Argernon's attention seemed to be focused on something beneath the bed. She watched his arms move but couldn't see what he was doing. He straightened, tossing what she now saw was a belt-like rope onto the mattress. It trailed off the edge, where she assumed it was somehow anchored to the bed. He held the other one as he walked to the other side. He crouched again and went back to work.

"Argernon? I'm not amused. Damn it, what are you doing? What are you planning?"

He stood when he'd finished, dropping the other rope on the other side of the bed. His intense gaze locked with hers. Casey knew she was in for a losing battle. She saw desire blazing in his eyes. She'd come to know that look well. He wanted her badly.

"Amusement has nothing to do with this. It's a lesson, Beautiful. I want you. I hurt for you. We need to be on the same level to understand each other. As long as *you* hurt, I hurt. As long as I hurt, you hurt. We will find common ground to build up from."

He got back on the bed. She kicked at him when he tried to grip her leg, getting in a solid punch to his chest. He grunted but didn't seem angry as he caught her foot in his large hand. He got between her thighs and Casey shouted her frustration as Argernon forced her leg to bend. He pushed her knee up toward her chest and held it, his other hand reaching for one of the belt ropes. She struggled harder but he managed to tie the soft material around her knee.

"Stop! I don't want to do this with you, Argernon."

He growled softly as he gripped her other leg. Casey fought again but he was just too strong. He carefully held her in place while he tied the belt around her other knee. Casey bucked, cursing at him. He'd tied her with her legs spread wide open. She could move her knees up and down a few inches but couldn't close them at all. It didn't hurt, but she was totally exposed to his sight.

And he was taking in the view.

Argernon's gaze was fixed on her displayed pussy. She stopped struggling after she realized it was turning him on even more to see her buck and wiggle in the restraints. She glared at him.

"Pervert."

"What is that?" He arched an eyebrow.

"A person who has sick sexual desires."

He chuckled. "My sexual desires are as healthy as they come. What would you like first? Would it be my fingers or my mouth, Beautiful?"

"Don't touch me."

He sighed. His hand reached for the lube container he'd left on the bed from earlier, when he'd gotten himself off. "I think fingers first. You can try to resist, but your body knows who it belongs to. My body only craves yours, just as your body only craves mine."

He spread the lube on his fingers. Casey was breathing fast. She clenched her teeth. "Damn it, Argernon. Don't do this. Please."

He met her eyes. "If I don't, you will leave me. I won't let you go. I cannot."

She tensed as he reached for her, squeezing her eyes shut, but she knew he was watching her face. His fingers coated with the cream were warm and wet. He ran his thumbs over her outer lips, spreading her wider.

She felt his hands shaking. It momentarily shocked her that he trembled.

"You are a pleasure to look at, Casey. You are so soft and pink."

Her teeth clenched together harder. His finger explored her slit then slid higher. Casey sucked in air as he started to play with her nub. She tried to ignore the sensation but the feeling was too good. She'd gone almost four days without his touch. She hadn't touched herself, either. Her clit throbbed at the attention it had been denied. She lifted her chin, turning her head away from him, trying so hard to hold still. She didn't mean to move her hips against his finger as he increased the pressure. They moved on their own.

He pushed a finger slowly inside her, testing her. He growled low and deep. "You're wet. I smell you, Casey. You respond perfectly to my touch."

"It's the lube," she hissed out.

"No. It's all you here." He withdrew a finger before he pushed in two of them slowly.

She bit her lip hard, trying to fight the moan that wanted to tear from her throat as his fingers slowly stretched her. He explored inside her as his other finger rubbed at her clit. Her hips bucked when his fingers pressed upward and he found the area inside her that finally forced a moan from between her lips.

She was going to come. Her inner muscles squeezed his moving fingers. He jerked his finger away from her clit but continued moving inside her. It felt damn good as he massaged her G-spot but without the pressure on her clit, her climax backed off slightly.

"Damn you," she panted.

"Tell me you want me."

She shook her head. "Never."

He growled. "Do you know how long I can make you burn for me, Beautiful?"

He eased his fingers out of her and Casey went limp on the bed. She was breathing heavily. Her body ached and throbbed with need. Argernon stretched over her, his hands braced on the bed at her sides. Their eyes locked when she looked up at him. They seemed to glow more than normal as passion flared in their depths. They were breathtaking as he studied her.

"I need you."

"Go to hell."

"Wherever that place is, it has to be better than where I am now, wanting you so badly even as you deny me."

He pulled back and Casey sagged with relief. She ached and her clit throbbed, but she'd won. He was giving up. She took deep breaths, trying to calm her body so her sexual frustration could ease—then her breath turned into a gasp when two large hands slid under her ass.

She lifted her head to see Argernon settling on the bed, holding her ass inches from the mattress. He slid his legs under hers and scooted closer. She had a bad feeling this wasn't over but couldn't stop herself from moaning with pleasure as he scooted even closer, his hard cock pressing against her slit.

His eyes met hers just as he moved his hips and began easing into her pussy. His thick cock pushed in slowly, making her feel as if she were in both heaven and hell as her body stretched to accept his thick length. Her wetness eased the way as Argernon pressed his pelvis against her inner thighs so he could get as close to her as possible.

He was buried balls deep inside her before he released her ass. Trailing his hands over her hips, up her stomach, he slid them back down to reach between her spread thighs. "I want to feel your release. I need you, Casey—and you need me."

She gasped as his fingers played with her. A moan tore from her lips. He was rubbing her clit as he slowly started to move his cock inside her. The sensation of him fucking her while he massaged her swollen nub was too much.

She gave up fighting him. This was a battle she didn't even want to win anymore.

She moaned loudly as her hips bucked against him. The man knew how to make her respond. She wasn't going to last. Argernon growled her name when he started to come. His cock swelled, getting larger, as his fingers strummed her clit faster.

Casey screamed out as the climax hit her. Argernon roared. Her inner muscles slammed tight around him, quaking, as his semen shot deep inside her. Their bodies locked together where they were joined as they both rode the pleasure.

Casey finally turned her head, panting, while her body started to come down from the blissful high.

"I love you, Beautiful," Argernon almost whispered.

Hot tears burned behind her eyelids, which she kept shut.

She wanted to say the words back. She just couldn't do it. Not yet. He'd let her walk into the mess his life was without even a warning. Earlier that day, a woman had been touching him sexually, and two others had been caressing his body. It didn't matter if he'd been unconscious and unable to refuse them. The image was still there in her head.

He slowly withdrew from her body. He untied the belts from her knees with very gentle hands and Casey shut her thighs when she was free, rolling to her side, away from him.

Argernon sighed as he stretched out next to her on the bed.

Long seconds passed in silence.

Then Argernon suddenly grabbed her, yanking her against his body.

Casey turned her head to stare at the man who'd just enfolded her in his arms. He held her so close that their skin was mashed together, yet his hold tightened even further. Their gazes met.

"I love you, Casey. Whatever it takes, I will make you know it is true."

She studied his eyes. He was a seriously stubborn man. He wasn't going to give up, and he truly wasn't going to let her go.

"What's your plan? Keep me tied to the bed? Keep trying to force me to want you?"

He sighed. "If that's what it takes. You're my bound, Casey. You belong to me. I belong to you. You own my thoughts and my emotions."

"It's just your body that's community property, right?"

He frowned. "You are trying to stir my anger and you cannot. I understand your words. No. My body is not available for other females. My body belongs to you alone."

"I'm tired, Argernon."

He nodded. "I know. I was told how you cared for me while I was unable to wake. Rever said he could see how strongly your emotions are for me. It means I know I have a chance of making you forgive me. I will,

Casey. I will never stop until you are smiling at me again, and you are willing in my arms. I miss you."

His words broke her heart just a bit more. She missed him too. An image flashed in her memory of her rushing into his arms that last day before the ship was attacked. He'd lifted her against his body and they'd kissed before they'd started to eat their meal. It had been so perfect, until that alarm had called him away.

She almost wished they could go back in time.

Chapter Thirteen

A hot mouth was licking her. Moans flew from her throat as that mouth sucked and tugged on her clit. She bucked her hips, pleasure coursing through her body. Two thick fingers slowly pushed into her, stretching her pussy. She cried out as she came hard around those digits as they drove in and out of her. They withdrew only after her walls stopped clenching around them.

Argernon's body came down on top of hers. He spread his thighs, forcing hers farther apart. Casey finally opened her eyes.

Sunshine streamed in through the bedroom window. She met his gaze as his thick cock nudged her soaked sex. Then he entered her with one fast thrust that stole her breath away.

Her arms tried to wrap around his neck but her hands wouldn't lower. Her wrists were still restrained to the headboard. She stared into his sexy eyes and wrapped her legs around his hips when he started to drive in and out of her in slow, deep thrusts.

Their gazes stayed locked together as Argernon fucked her. She moaned, wrapping her legs higher around his waist, until her feet dug into his muscular ass. She could feel his muscles flexing under her heels with each deep penetration. He rolled his hips, changing the position he hit inside her just right, and Casey had to shut her eyes.

"Yes!"

"There?" He growled at her in that sexy tone she loved.

He moved again to hit the same spot. Casey frantically nodded and clung to him with her legs. Her fingers wrapped around the chains that moored her to the headboard, hanging on for dear life. The hair on Argernon's chest brushed her nipples, making her moan louder with the sensory overload.

When he lowered his face and kissed her neck, nipping at the skin along her shoulder with his sharp fangs, she lost it. She came hard again, her muscles clamping around Argernon.

He groaned, biting a little harder as he jerked deep inside her and came.

"That was so unfair. I wasn't awake."

He released her skin with a chuckle. "I can never be fair where you are concerned, Beautiful. I will do anything to keep you here in my arms where you belong."

Casey stared at him. He was clearly amused. She couldn't help the very small, reluctant smile she offered back. "You're not off the hook yet, Baby."

He grinned. "*You* are not off the..." His head rose and he eyed her wrists and then looked back at her. "The headboard yet."

"So that really *is* your master plan? Keep me chained to your bed, seducing me, until I forgive you?"

He grinned. "Will it work?"

"Is there food involved, and a shower?"

He laughed. "Yes."

"Let me go."

His smile died. "Never."

She studied his intense expression and the stubbornness in the way he looked at her fiercely. "I meant, let my wrists free. Please?"

He studied her. "Will you try to run away from me? I won't let you out of my sight." His voice dropped to a deeper tone. "You know I will do anything to keep you."

"Yes. I know you will. Right now, I'm just hungry and I want a shower. I'm not plotting my escape. Not yet anyway."

He laughed as he slowly lifted off her, withdrawing from her body. He rolled away to get off the bed and Casey watched him grab something off the nightstand. Their gazes met when he reached over the bed to free each wrist. She sat up, rubbing them, and Argernon held out a hand to her.

"We'll shower before we eat. The new house helper should have arrived at first light. You will like her. She will wear clothing in the house; I know you will appreciate this. Her name is Gava, and she finds humans fascinating. She and Ariel get along well."

Casey sighed. "Where did she come from?"

"My father's household."

Casey flushed. "She was with your father? They were lovers?"

He shook his head. "Her bound died recently and she was staying at my father's home until she could find a new one. When a bound dies, his family or his friends take his women into their household, to protect them until they find new homes or, if they are old, to live out their remaining days. My father has a full house and Gava loved her bound. She wanted no other male in her life, so coming into our home is perfect for her. She is very fond of me and I am very fond of her."

Casey frowned. "*How* fond?"

Argernon laughed. "She is like a mother, and I am like her son. She gave her bound two daughters but no sons. You will meet her and feel no jealousy, Casey."

"Okay."

He smiled as he helped her up, keeping hold of her hand as he led her into the bathroom. They showered quickly together and Casey brushed her teeth while Argernon shaved. Zorn grew hair on their lower jaw that she assumed all of them tended. She'd not seen a male yet with facial hair, except when Argernon was injured and hadn't been able to remove it. She almost missed the hair there. It had looked good on him.

He smiled as she watched him. "What are you thinking?"

"I liked the hair along your jaw when it grew out. It looked very sexy."

He laughed. "Only very old men let it grow. I'm a warrior. We keep our faces clean of hair to show we are respectful of our elders."

"Is that a Zorn custom?"

He nodded. "Zorn males who do not shave are…" He hesitated before saying, "Not respectful, and do not follow the laws well. Most of them end up locked away for crimes."

"Wow."

He brushed his teeth before leading her back to the bedroom. He dressed in just pants and handed her one of his soft black shirts to put on.

"I will buy you clothing. It will take a few days, but Gava will shop for you."

"What does Gava do here? What will *my* responsibilities be?"

"Gava will do the shopping, the cooking and the cleaning. She will tend to your needs and make sure you are not lonely when I am not home. You can help her if you wish." He glanced at her. "You are my bound. You are to be pampered and you are house lead."

"I heard that the term before; Bara mentioned it."

"It means you are in charge."

Casey grinned. "Do I get to order *you* around?" She tugged the shirt down her body, where it fell halfway her thighs. She eyed her bare legs. "Can I borrow pants?"

He chuckled. "No. Bound women walk naked in the home, but you are very covered. I want to at least see your legs, Beautiful. It is a fair compromise, is it not?"

"So you never answered my question. Do I get to order you around?"

His look sparkled with amusement. "What do you wish me to do? We'll see if I will take your orders."

Her naughty side flared as she took in his mostly naked body. He was a prime specimen of man. Just looking at him made her want to touch him, despite the hurt still causing her doubt.

Her gaze paused at the front of his pants. She couldn't miss the bulge there. He was hard again. "Open your pants."

His eyebrows rose but a grin spread on his lips as he reached for his waist. He opened his pants. His cock sprang free and she eyed it with a smile. The man was built.

She wiggled her finger at him. "Come here."

He walked slowly toward her. She saw desire burning in his eyes as he inched closer. He stopped a foot away, staring down at her.

The fact that he was taking orders was surprising...and it really turned her on. He was a big tough guy, but he was doing everything she said. Their gazes met as Casey slowly sank to her knees. Argernon growled, his cock jerked in front of her face, advertising his excitement.

Casey reached out to stroke the underside of his shaft with her fingers. Argernon's legs tensed as he braced them.

"Hold really still. Don't move unless I tell you to."

He groaned. "I won't move."

Licking her lips to wet them, she cupped his balls. "Spread your legs farther apart."

He did. It amazed Casey that he was letting her get away with this. He was usually so damn bossy and in charge.

She breathed on the head of his cock, making it jerk again. A growl rumbled from deep in his throat. She licked the head before opening her mouth wide, taking him in as deep as she dared without choking...

And felt movement.

She jerked away, looking up. His hand hovered by her head.

"You moved."

"I wanted to touch your hair."

She shook her head. "No. Put your hands on your thighs. Keep them there."

He growled but did it, his eyes narrowed.

She smiled, turning her focus back to his cock. She opened her mouth once more and stroked him with her tongue while sucking on him. His balls tightened. He was so keyed up, she knew he wouldn't last long. She also knew he really loved this. He became so turned on that he couldn't hold back.

When he started to shake, she released his cock with her mouth to gaze up at him.

Argernon looked ready to explode. His eyes were glazed over with lust. He had sweat beaded on his forehead and his hands were fisted at his sides. He was breathing hard, his fangs peeking between his parted lips.

"Lie on the bed."

"Casey—"

"Lie on the bed. I want you on your back."

He groaned in protest but started walking. She was amazed again that he was listening. She watched him kick off his pants before getting on the bed and rolling over so he was flat on his back. His breath was labored and his cock was pulsing from need.

She kept the shirt on as she climbed onto the mattress after him. She moved closer, on her knees, letting her eyes slowly trace every inch of him before she threw a leg over his waist. She lifted the shirt so her bare ass rested on his lower stomach. His cock was pressed against the seam of her ass.

She shoved the shirt out of the way and kept her eyes on Argernon as she reached down, lifting up a few inches to put her hand between her thighs. She was so wet. She rubbed her fingers through her lower lips, wetting them then rubbing her clit.

Argernon had his full attention fixed on her fingers and what they were doing. He started breathing even harder.

"Do I have your attention, Baby?"

His eyes flew to hers. "Yes."

She rubbed her clit faster, but watching him get turned on excited her even more. His hot gaze returned to her vee, watching avidly as she rubbed her clit with her fingertips. She reached behind her with her other hand, gripping his cock. Argernon sucked in air loudly while she positioned him so she could ease down.

She moaned as he filled her. Her pussy expanded snuggly to accept him. His hands gripped her thighs, a snarl tearing from his throat.

"Lord of the Moons! That feels the best…"

She rode him hard while rubbing her clit. She was going to come. She knew *he* was going to come as well.

She suddenly stopped riding him but she kept fingering her nub.

"Baby?"

His eyes met hers.

"Don't ever hurt me again. You're good at seducing me...but I'm no slouch in that department either. Do you want to come?"

"Please!"

She lifted up and twisted her hips as she slammed down, driving him into her deeper.

Argernon roared, throwing his head back, clawing at the bed. He came hard, his hips bucking under her. She pressed on her clit crying out as she climaxed. Her back arched at the intensity of it.

She collapsed on his chest when the last of the pleasure moved through her.

Argernon wrapped his arms around her, gripping her ass in his hands. They were both breathing hard. His palms caressed her backside as a deep rumbling chuckle came from him.

Casey lifted her head to look at him. "I take it that you're not mad?"

"No. What is a slouch?"

She grinned. "It means I'm good at seducing you too."

"Beautiful, you could just smile at me and I would want to be buried inside you deep."

"Well, if that's the case, I won't bother asking you to open your pants anymore, or give you a show of playing with myself while I ride you."

"Please do." He grinned.

She laughed. "Okay. Only if you follow orders from time to time and ask really nicely." Sitting up, she removed the shirt, too hot with it on. "So what can I order you to do next? I have a few ideas."

Argernon rolled suddenly, pinning her down under his body. "I would—"

Their bedroom door opened suddenly.

Casey gasped. They were both naked, Argernon was on top of her, and they were fused together since he was still deep inside her body. She turned her head—

To see Bara framed in the doorway gripping a wicked-looking knife.

It was big and sharp, and horror hit Casey as the woman advanced.

Argernon sighed, not even looking. "Gava, *never* enter our room. Casey is shy about—"

Casey used every ounce of strength to shove at Argernon.

She managed to knock him off her and screamed out a warning. Argernon saw the danger as he landed on his side, and a roar exploded from his lips as he grabbed Casey. He rolled with her so they both fell off the opposite side of the high bed.

Casey landing hard on top of him—and heard a *crack*. She stared down at Argernon's face in horror.

His eyes were closed.

"You humans think you can just take our men!" Bara yelled.

Casey got to her feet. Argernon didn't move and he didn't open his eyes but she knew he was breathing. He must have hit his head hard enough to knock him out, but she prayed that sound didn't mean something even worse.

She stared across the massive bed at Bara, who stood on the other side, knife in hand, growling at her.

"I was with Argis Ral, serving in his household. That human weakling tricked him into bounding her while he was captured by an enemy." Bara inched toward the end of the bed, glaring at Casey. "He gave me to Argis Argernon, who promised me that he wouldn't give me to another household. But he was tricked by *you*. I will not be removed from another household! The house I chose is not an Argis home."

The woman looked unhinged as she continued to stalk closer. "I don't have my own room. The male is not as skilled at sex as Argis Argernon. He can't buy me the things I want because he keeps a *budget*." She spat the word. "I want my household back—and you can't be bound to Argis Argernon if you are *dead*. If he does not like it, he will die with you! I will not give up my high station!"

Casey swallowed hard, silently staring at the knife-wielding bitch who was obviously totally nuts, trying to decide her next play. Bara was a lot taller and stronger.

Argernon's leg moved and he groaned slightly. He was coming around. He reached for the back of his head to rub it as his eyes opened. He frowned, exploring the back of his head as Casey's gaze flew back to Bara.

She was a danger to both Argernon and this woman.

If Argernon himself didn't die at Bara's hand, he wasn't going to let Bara get away with killing her. Casey knew that. He would gut the bitch with the very knife she used on Casey if Bara killed her.

Casey took a deep breath—then she did the last thing the crazy Zorn woman expected. She screamed and launched her body at the bigger woman.

Surprise widened the woman's eyes in the seconds before Casey tackled her, grabbing the arm with the knife with both hands even as their bodies slammed brutally together.

They both went down in a heap. Casey landed on top of Bara, and she knew the wind was knocked out of her by the loud gasp and Bara's face paling instantly.

Casey didn't hesitate for a second. She lifted her knee, ramming it between Bara's thighs, *hard*.

The woman screamed. Male or female, Casey knew that fucking hurt. The knife dropped from Bara's fingers so Casey could shove it away, where it slid under the bed.

Hauling back her fist, Casey decked her in the nose with everything she had.

Pain shot up her arm but she hauled her fist back to punch Bara again. She saw blood this time. Bara screamed. Casey grabbed a handful of the woman's hair and used it to ram her head against the floor before punching Bara again in the face.

Two large hands grabbed Casey around her torso and she was pulled off the screaming Zorn woman. Casey jerked her head around to stare wildly at Argernon. He adjusted his hold, covering her breasts and her groin with his big arms, and then lifted Casey off her feet, hugging her body to his while he backed them across the room, away from the woman on the floor.

Bara curled into a ball where she lay, sobbing between cries of pain. Her nose was bleeding and both of her hands were cupping her groin.

The sound of pounding boots penetrated Casey's brain about the same time that Argernon cursed, spinning Casey around and pinning her to the wall. His body almost smashed hers but at least her front was fully covered by his. She could see over his shoulder as four Zorn men dressed in black rushed into the room.

They looked at the woman on the floor before their stares jerked to Argernon.

A man with red hair snarled. "What is happening here?"

Argernon growled. "That was my lead house helper until she went to another home yesterday. She did not like that I bound to a human, and no longer had a need for other women in my home. She came here with a knife. It is under the bed, where it slid away during the fight. She no longer had a right to be in my home. She has trespassed. She has also attacked me and my bound with threats of death."

The redhead's gaze flew to the woman on the floor and then back. His body relaxed slightly. He frowned at Argernon. "Did you have to damage her so much, Argis Argernon? I understand your anger but she is female. This is unacceptable."

Argernon sighed. "I hit my head. I was knocked out. It was my bound who fought her."

The man's stared at Casey as shock transformed his features. "Present her for inspection."

Argernon growled. "She's bare. That is why I am holding her here, to cover her body from sight."

The man nodded, examining the room. He walked to the dresser, found a shirt, then walked back and draped the shirt on Argernon's shoulder. He turned to jerk a nod toward the other men. Two of them stepped close to Bara, guarding her, but they turned their backs to Casey and Argernon.

Argernon lowered Casey to the floor to help put the shirt on her, tugging it down her body while staring into her eyes.

"Am I in trouble? She had a knife." Fear crept through her. She didn't know their laws. "Are they going to arrest me?"

Argernon shook his head. "Just do as he says. I'm here, Casey."

She was shaking as she stepped around Argernon.

The four large Zorn officers turned an openly studied Casey but the redhead was obviously in charge. His gaze ran down her quickly before he addressed Argernon.

"May I, with respect?"

Argernon gave a short nod. "Yes. Hold still, Casey. He is checking you for injuries or markings to support your claim that you were in a fight."

She tensed as the big man approached her. He was clearly unconvinced that she'd fought Bara, judging by the disbelieving look on his face. He hesitated before lowering to his knees, which left them almost eye to eye.

He held out both of his hands, palms up. "Please put your hands in mine."

She was shaking but she allowed his gentle hold. He stared at her hands. She had blood on both. Her right knuckles were damaged from when she'd hit Bara a few times.

The man released her hands then visually scanned her again, from her toes up to her forehead. He was still frowning.

"Do you have any other injures?"

"I don't think so. I took her by surprise. She didn't expect me to tackle her. She probably expected me to run away instead."

The redhead's eyebrows arched. "You leapt at her?"

"I threw myself into her as hard as I could to knock her down."

The man cleared his throat, looking astonished. "Explain how she was injured, please."

Casey sighed. "I slammed my knee into her crotch. It hurts regardless of what sex you are. I deck—uh...punched her in the face until she dropped the knife, and slammed her head into the floor because I knew if she got up before I disabled her, she'd kick my ass. She's a lot bigger than I am. I only had surprise on my side."

"Crotch?"

"Um, her…" Casey turned, looking at Argernon for help. "What do you call it?"

Argernon bit back a laugh. "She hit Bara's sex with her knee."

"Thanks." Casey met the redhead's eyes. "That's what I did. She wanted to kill me. She threatened to kill Argernon. He already has a head injury from an attack on the ship we arrived on, and then he hit his head again when he rolled us off the bed to keep Bara from stabbing us. He needs medical help."

Her glance went to Bara, who was still whimpering, still curled in a ball on the floor. "And so does Bara. I might have broken her nose. I felt something crunch."

The redhead climbed to his feet, gaping at Casey. He turned to Argernon. "I have been told human females are weak. She's so little. Her bones are so small and…" He shook his head. "Amazing."

Argernon pulled Casey back into his arms, curling his naked body around her back to hold her close. She looked up at him. He was grinning at the redheaded officer.

"She is smaller but fierce. There is a lot more to human women than you would think."

The redhead nodded. "I will remove the intruder from your home. She tried to kill you. Do you want to press full charges, Argis Argernon?"

Argernon's grin died. "I do. She poses a threat to my bound. I won't have that. She knew how to sneak into my home to attack us in our bed. Make sure it doesn't happen again."

The man nodded. "Do you need medical?"

"I'm fine."

Casey frowned, looking up at Argernon. "You need to see a doctor."

He sighed. "I am fine, Casey."

She shook her head. "*Fine*. I'll wait until you fall down and then a doctor can look at you when you're passed out cold. Of all the stubborn, stupid things men do..."

He chuckled as the redhead gasped in astonishment. His gaze was darting from Argernon to Casey and back.

Argernon laughed harder. "They are also very willful. It is amusing. She is a pleasure in all things. I could not resist her."

The redhead backed away slowly. He nodded but he looked uncertain. "I would train her better, Argis Argernon. Otherwise she might rub off on our women. They would all try to tell us what to do."

Argernon looked at Casey with a sparkle in his eye. "You would be surprised at how pleasurable it is to follow a woman's orders in the bedroom."

She grinned at him. He *had* enjoyed her telling him what to do when she'd seduced him. She tore her gaze from his as the men lifted a still-crying Bara from the floor. Two of them carried her out. The other man crawled under the bed to retrieve the knife and all of them left.

An older woman rushed into the room right after.

Casey stared at who she assumed was Gava. The woman was six feet tall, had to be eighty if she was a day, judging by the wrinkles on her face, but was in amazing health. Age hadn't bent her back or softened her firm body that was revealed. Her silver hair was long, nearly reaching her knees, and she wore a sleeveless dress. The woman rushed for them both.

"Are you all right? I called for security when I heard the shouting. She tied a cord from my door to another, to lock me in my room. Thankfully I have an alarm in there. I was worried." The woman seemed to not notice or care that Argernon was naked. All of her attention was on Casey. She smiled. "You are very attractive."

Casey grinned. "Thank you for getting help to us. And thank you for the compliment."

The woman laughed. She finally turned her attention on Argernon, shaking her head, taking in what she could see of him behind Casey. "It is a good thing our males are not shy." She made a soft sound with her throat. "Get dressed, please. I do not want to see so much of you."

She spun away. "Food is prepared. Hurry to come eat. Your bound is with offspring and needs much food to fatten her up. She is so small that we need to make her bigger, so she has an easier time birthing a big, healthy Zorn baby."

Chapter Fourteen

"She likes you."

Casey turned in Argernon's arms. "What's going to happen to Bara?"

"You don't want to know."

"I hate when you say that. Give it to me straight."

He hesitated. "She will be treated for mental instability and sent to where she won't harm anyone again. If she refuses treatment and punishment, then she will be sent to a med house."

Casey paled. "Oh. That's one of those places they send women to help sick males with sex, isn't it?"

"She tried to kill you." Argernon's features hardened, rage burning in his furious look. "If she had been male, I would have killed her with my bare hands for coming after you. It is my right. Even if security arrived, if she were male, I could kill her in front of them for coming after my bound. She is lucky she is female. Death isn't an option for her. She would have killed you, and our offspring, so do not think about what she has done to her own life. She will be given options but she must pay for her crime."

"How's your head? I wish you'd go see Ahhu."

He shook his head. "I am unhurt." A grin curved his lips. "I am proud of you. You fought well."

"I fought dirty. I was scared she was going to kick my ass and kill both of us."

He laughed. "You were fierce. You struck without pause and you took down your adversary." His grin died. "Now do not ever do it again. I will strive to protect you better so you never have to defend yourself. You will remember that you are small and carrying my offspring."

Her hand went to her stomach. "I don't plan on any more fights. I didn't plan on *that* one."

He nodded. "Where did you learn to fight? Is that common on Earth? Do they train all humans to be warriors?"

She laughed. "No. I was raised with a lot of boy family members. They liked to pick on me so I learned to fight dirty to get even."

Rage crossed Argernon's features. "Tell me who they are and I will go to Earth to punish every male who has harmed you."

She stared up at him, dazed when she realized he meant it. He wanted to go to Earth to kick some ass for her benefit. She smiled, reaching up to cup his face.

"You are so sweet."

He frowned. "I am not sweet. I want to harm all males who caused you to learn how to fight to defend yourself. I will schedule transportation to Earth immediately and make them suffer."

She tried hard not to laugh. "'Picking on' is…well, no one hurt me. They teased me and they pissed me off, but they didn't physically harm me."

He growled. "I don't want to hear about men teasing you. I want to kill men who touched you."

She had to fight back another laugh. "It wasn't sexual. Teasing is making a joke at someone else's expense that they don't find funny."

Finally his body relaxed. "I understand. So there are no men on Earth I should do harm to?"

"Just my ex-boyfriend. He's the guy who sent those two men to arrest me. He's not worth the time or the trip to Earth." She leaned against Argernon, smiling up at him. "Besides, I don't want to go on another damn ship ever again."

"Food!" Gava bellowed from the other side of the house.

Argernon chuckled. "Did I mention she is like a mother? She sounds like one."

"You did. And I *am* starving."

He released her to dress quickly in a pair of pants. He put a shirt on this time too. "Come, Beautiful."

She loved it when he called her that. She wasn't beautiful, no one had ever called her that before, but he looked like he meant it every time he said it. Maybe to Zorn men, she was. It was a nice feeling.

Gava was waiting for them in a dining room and they sat down to a heavily filled table of food. Halfway through the meal, a buzzer sounded.

"What was that?" Casey looked around the room for the source of the sound.

Argernon stood up. "Someone is at the front door. I will get it."

Casey watched him walk away, hoping that it wasn't going to be another pissed-off ex-house helper. One visit from Bara was more than enough.

Seconds later, Ariel and her husband rushed into the dining room. Ariel looked angry—and so did her large husband, who was glaring at Argernon.

"Are you all right? I woke up to find you hadn't come to the house. We went to the medical building but they told us you left last night, so we tracked you down here." Ariel shot Argernon a nasty look. "Someone bribed the guards to bring you *here* instead of to my house. You wouldn't know anything about that, would you, Argernon?"

He grinned as he sat back down. "I am guilty. I made them bring my bound home to me."

"It's all right," Casey said softly.

Ariel's eyebrows shot up as she hugged her rounded stomach. "Really? You made up?"

Ral, her husband, smiled. "I told you that it would be fine."

Ariel shot her husband a look. "If he's anything like you, she didn't stand a chance." Ariel sat down, glancing at Gava. "May I? I'm always hungry. I swear this baby eats three times what I do. I go around in a constant state of starvation. If it wasn't for my workouts I'd be as big as this house."

A smiling Gava made a heaping plate to set in front of Ariel. "Zorn offspring are like that for women. It must be a boy." Gava shot both men a grin. "Their appetites in all things are extreme, and they can't get enough from any woman who holds them in their bodies."

Casey almost choked on her food. Ariel laughed. "Get used to it. They're blunt like that. It's a common theme to joke about what horndogs Zorn men are."

Argernon frowned. "What is a horndog?"

"You." Ariel pointed to her husband. "Him. It means you can't get enough sex. You always want it."

Argernon grinned as his gaze went to Casey. "I am definitely a horndog then."

Ral chuckled as he took a seat next to his wife, stealing a piece of fruit from her plate. She winked at him, obviously amused. Love shone in her eyes and it was clear he was just as crazy about her.

Casey observed the couple. They were starkly contrasted. Ariel was small where her husband was big. Ariel was pale in coloring where her husband was deeply tan. They were happy together and very much in love.

Her gaze went to Argernon. He was watching her silently.

"What are you thinking?" His voice was soft.

She shook her head. "It's nothing worth sharing."

"I *always* find myself wanting to know what you are thinking." He frowned.

Ral chuckled. "Your life will change in many ways, brother." He looked fondly at his wife before turning his attention on Casey. "We aren't used to this kind of relationship with women. Zorn women are quiet and they keep to themselves. Women socialize with other women. Most socialization happens between males and females in the bedroom. Even there, not much conversation is exchanged. But human women interact with us on all levels. You speak to us about many things and keep our interest."

His gaze went back to Ariel. "I want to spend all my time with my Ariel. She engages me in every way, at all times."

Ariel winked at Casey. "I'm almost terrified when I think of how many kids we're going to end up with. Birth control doesn't work with them. Their semen, I've been told, gets around every form of birth control they try."

"What about condoms?"

Ariel's eyes widened. "Explain to Argernon what one is. This should be amusing." She shot her husband a look. "Don't say a word."

Ral laughed. He popped another piece of fruit in his mouth, giving a nod of encouragement to Casey before he watched his brother expectantly.

Sighing, Casey faced Argernon. "A condom is a soft, stretchy material that fits over your cock, from tip to base, and it catches your seed so it doesn't enter a woman. Do you understand?"

Argernon snarled. He stood up so fast his chair tumbled several feet and he looked petrified as he stared at Casey. He shook his head as he backed away. "NO!"

She was stunned by his reaction. She'd expected something funny. This wasn't amusing. Argernon looked horrified. He was staring at her like she'd just asked him to cut off his own nuts with a rusty knife.

She shot Ariel an angry frown.

Ariel nodded. "Tell her why you won't wear a condom."

Casey eyed Argernon. He still looked pissed off and insulted. "When Zorn males are young—"

"Teenagers," Ariel interjected. "Really horny teenagers."

Argernon took a deep breath. "We have little control over our sexual urges at that age. If left unchecked, a younger male will..." He sighed. "He will spend most of his time issuing self-release. He will never learn to control his sexual desires."

Ariel laughed. "They'll actually jerk off until they can't walk and get dehydrated, from what I've understood."

With a sharp nod, Argernon glared at Ariel and then met Casey's eyes again. "In order to teach males control, and so we do not self-release over and over all day long, we are fitted with a device that sounds like what you mentioned. It is tight and with no room for release. If a male releases into one, there is nowhere for his seed to go." He cleared his throat. "It is very painful."

Casey stared at him. She didn't laugh. That wasn't funny. "Why would you let anyone do that to you?"

It was Ral who explained. "We need to learn control over our bodies. It is hard to begin training or do anything productive if all our males are self-releasing constantly." He smiled. "I learned control fast, but some males…" His gaze went to Argernon, and Ral smirked. "Some males did not, did they, brother? How many times were you found on the floor of your room in pain?"

Argernon growled. "Shut up."

Ral laughed. He told Casey, "It was many, many times."

Casey stared at Argernon. Sympathy for the teenage boy he must have been welled in her. "Why didn't you just take it off?"

He sighed. "Because they cannot be tampered with; they give an even more painful shock if you try to remove them. They are only removed for bathing and urine release, with an adult Zorn present to make sure that is all that is done. Three times a day, young males are allowed sexual release. I wanted more."

"I'm hoping for a girl," Ariel said.

Casey nodded. "No shit." She stared at Argernon. "There's room in condoms for release, and they don't hurt you. They just catch your seed."

He shivered. "I will never again wear something that embraces me like that." His eyes narrowed on her. "Only *you* embrace my cock." He offered a sexy grin. "I will wear you often."

Casey blushed, a little surprised that he'd say something that forward in front of other people.

Ariel laughed. "Like I said, they're very blunt." Ariel stood up, giving a smile to her husband. "Let's go home. All is well here."

Casey watched the couple leave...knowing she could ask Ariel to take her with them.

She remained silent until they were out of sight.

Argernon was watching her. She turned, studying him back. A slow grin spread his lips. "You did not try to escape." He sounded smug.

"Would you have let me go?"

He shook his head. "You are my bound, Beautiful. I will never let you go."

"Why would she want free?" Gava looked at Casey with a frown. "Why would you not want bound to him? He is much desired on Zorn. He is Argis. Many Zorn women would beg to be his bound."

"It's a long story," Casey sighed. Her gaze went to Argernon. "You're still not off the hook."

He chuckled. "And later, you still will not be off the headboard."

Gava stood. "I do not want to know." She started to clear the table. When Casey rose to help her, Gava shook her head. "You remain with your bound. You are in the beginning stages of your new bond. Enjoy the time together." She disappeared from the dining room.

"You heard her." Argernon moved to Casey. "Let's go enjoy our time together." He held out his hand.

"Gee, I wonder what you want to do." Her gaze lowered to the front of his pants. The man was hard again. She put her smaller hand in his. "Are you ever *not* turned on?"

He chuckled. "When you are not near me, I am not aroused…unless I am thinking about you. I want to take you outside right now. You have yet to enjoy Zorn."

"That's true. When we arrived, I was chasing after you to the medical place and when I left there, it was dark."

He walked her through the house but instead of heading for the front of the house, he headed toward the back, to a set of glass doors that he slid open. The view of the city below was vast. The house sat on a steep hill, so she could look down the sharply slanted lawn to see a lot of Zorn. Tall white walls enclosed an expansive backyard below them. She let her eyes take in the view.

Zorn really *was* a red planet. The vegetation she saw wasn't green. It was all reds, purples, and blacks. The sky was a pinkish hue. The city was mostly white buildings that looked rounded and curved. She was far enough away that she couldn't see people or much detail, but she bet it would be pretty at night with lights below. The grass was a rich purple that shocked her a little with its color. Zorn definitely wasn't Earth.

"What do you think?"

"It's stunning and strange," she said honestly. "It's really different from Earth."

He nodded. "I was on your Earth, remember?"

She looked up at him. "I remember in great detail."

He chuckled. "I liked your blue and green water."

"I liked the cave behind the waterfall on your sleeping bag."

His grin curved more. "I was trying to give you a rest but I don't believe you need one, since your thoughts are on our first joining." He turned her to yank her against his body. "I want you."

"Let's go inside."

He shook his head. "No one is here. Gava will not interfere."

"Its broad daylight and we're on a hill, Argernon."

"I am aware."

He went to his knees, tugging her down with him. She stared up at him. The guy turned her on so badly. "What if Gava walks by the windows?"

"She won't watch us. Sex is very natural here, my Casey. She will avoid the windows."

Biting her lip, Casey stared into Argernon's striking blue eyes.

She loved him. Deeply.

When Bara tried to kill them both, it was glaringly clear the woman hadn't loved Argernon. She wanted what he could give her financially, she wanted his status. He hadn't broken anyone's heart by getting rid of his house helpers. He'd just hurt Casey by having them in the first place...a cultural difference she'd have to come to terms with on her own time.

Argernon reached up to cup Casey's face in his hands. "I love you, Beautiful."

"I love you too, Baby."

"Turn around."

She went to her hands and knees, facing the city. Argernon moved behind her, spreading his bent legs so they were on the outside of hers. His warm body pressed against her back.

One of his hands caressed her stomach gently before lowering to the hem of her shirt, pulling it up and out of his way. His fingers slid between her thighs. Casey moaned as he played with her clit.

Argernon lowered his head so his mouth could tease her neck. "You're more beautiful than the view. I can never lose you, Casey."

She pressed her ass back, rubbing against his hard cock trapped in his pants. He groaned as she wiggled against him. "I'll forgive you for everything, and stay here with you forever...if you do one thing."

His hand froze. "What? Name it, Casey."

She looked at him over her shoulder, meeting his sexy eyes. "Swear to me you'll never touch any woman but me for the rest of our lives together."

He nodded. "I swear. You are all that I want. You are all that I need. You are everything to me."

"Will you occasionally take orders from me?"

He smiled. "Yes."

"Then open those damn pants and fuck me."

Argernon chuckled. "Do you want me fast or slow, Beautiful? Tell me."

She bent lower, placing her elbows on the purple grass of Zorn. "Slow at first, and then fast. That's how I love it best."

He growled at her. "You are perfect for me."

She tossed her brown hair out of the way to look at him over her shoulder again. "Play with my clit while you fuck me, and you'll be perfect for *me*." She grinned.

Argernon shoved his pants down. He entered her slowly. Casey shut her eyes, reveling in the feel of the man she loved moving inside her. Yeah, she could do this for the rest of her life, happily, as long as she had Argernon.

Muscular arms slid around her. A hot hand slid between her thighs. Argernon's finger rubbed against her clit as he pushed into her deep.

Being bound to Argernon would be sheer pleasure.

He started to move faster. Casey moaned. "Love me, Baby."

"Always, Beautiful." He chuckled. "And often. Very, very often."

20525940R00144

Printed in Great Britain
by Amazon